ASTRID CORTEZ AND THE MIDNIGHT CORONATION

A Novel

DAGOBERTO PÉREZ

STRANGE
RIVER

For my Lori, Ana and Olivia Grace.

Bad Magic

"MAGIC ISN'T JUST for witches," snapped Astrid Cortez. Growing up, she'd heard people compare her grandmother, who was a healer, or *curandera,* to a witch. She hated the confusion between the two. Oblivious to his blunder, Benny Felton used his phone as a mirror to fix his blue hair. "Girl, all I know is that witches use magic and witches are bad."

Their walk back home from the Saturday photography session at the old cemetery had led them through the heart of their hometown of Diller, a rural South Texas farming town located by the Rio Grande River. Astrid glanced down at the caliche road, nudging her glasses back up her petite nose. She found herself wondering why on earth she'd agreed to help Benny with his photography homework. As they made their way across Cenizo Road, the neighborhood dogs began barking. Reacting to the noise, Benny feigned throwing rocks at them. "Beat it! I'm the only bitch around here," he boasted as they scattered.

Despite her annoyance, Astrid couldn't help but laugh. She regarded her tall, flamboyant best friend, wearing a yellow "Always Camera Ready" shirt. Benny was too self-involved for true malice.

It wasn't apparent at first, but Benny came from money. Ranchland and Texas cattle money. He wasn't a Rockefeller or a DuPont, but his family was about as ritzy as it got in South Texas. The Felton's were politicians, and they had schools named after them. Any other boy looking or acting like Benny

1

would be an outcast. Benny's money and family name granted him celebrity status in Border Town USA, as long as no one talked about the fact that little Benny Felton liked boys. He was funny. He was an Artist. He was sensitive and silly. But don't you dare call Benny a queer. That was dangerous territory. The Felton's influence was long and their memory even longer.

Astrid finally spoke up, "People mistake card readers, *curanderas*, and healers as witches, categorizing them all as *brujas*. My mom and grandma are not evil - they just have special abilities. If people call them witches, then so be it. I'm still proud of my roots."

Benny swatted a bug away from his face. "Jeez, calm down Malcolm Hex, I only brought it up because I remembered my mom got upset when she found out we were going to take pictures at the cemetery today. She warned me I'd see a *bruja* if I went with you. I told her we were just going to the cemetery for a school project, but she was still fuming." His voice climbed an octave as he mimicked his mother: "Why go there with her? You know what she and her family are—she went on and on. I ended up just lying and saying I wasn't coming so she'd shut up. She thinks I'm home right now. That's why I didn't bring my car. You think I like walking Dante's First Level of Hell with you?" he pointed at the dilapidated town around him.

"We're not witches, especially not me. What do you think my powers are? Am I going to turn into an owl and eat her?"Astrid rolled her eyes.

"You know my mom's not well. I wouldn't worry about it. Hey—" he shifted the conversation. "Let me see the photos you took. I want to see if I'm going to get an A. I need a hundred at this point."

"I think there are twenty good ones." Astrid removed the camera dangling from her neck and handed it over to Benny, who snatched it incredulously.

"I'll be the judge of that," Benny remarked, flipping through the images. "Good. OK. Hmm. No. I don't like that one. Good. Oooooooohhh," he stopped on a photo, turning the camera towards Astrid. "And this?"

A photo of their classmate, Dylan Arias, appeared before her. Astrid's eyes widened as she quickly seized the camera back.

"Girl, make sure you don't send me that one. Unless you want me to use that *papi chulo* as part of the 'Beauty in Decay' assignment," cackled Benny.

Astrid snapped, "Shut your face," then swiftly deleted the photo. "Did you like the photos or not?"

"Yeah, they'll do. Just send them to my email so I can upload them to the class website. I can't afford to fail again. Dude!" he exclaimed suddenly, bounding into another train of thought: "Did you see the pictures of Abigail that were posted on the class website? That heifer has gained so much weight since getting pregnant!"

"How ridiculous," replied Astrid. "She's sixteen. My mom would kill me if I got pregnant in high school—fetus and all."

"Honestly, at this point I think my mom would be thrilled if I got a girl pregnant."

"Your mom's got issues," said Astrid. "Having a kid won't make you straight."

"Tell me about it. Mom was telling me about a church where they cure people of what she calls 'those thoughts.' Mexico has a few, apparently. And there's one not too far from here. Dummy doesn't realize I like the *papi chulos*."

"Oh my God," Astrid chortled. "Shut up. You're all talk. One wink from a hot Mexican guy and you'd crap your pants."

Without missing a beat, Benny quipped, "Oh yeah, cause you've got guys banging down your door." He feigned resentment and scoffed, "At least I try to talk to guys."

"I'm a work-in-progress," she replied, wanting to change the subject. "You better pick up your grade with these photos. I don't want to end up doing more of your homework for you."

"Yeah, I really can't be meeting you like this anymore anyway. Like I said, Her-Royal- Pain-in-my-Side Regina Felton doesn't want me talking to you anymore. I have to lie to her whenever I go out with you."

"Why?"

"She thinks you made me gay."

Astrid stopped walking. "Me? Why me? Has she met you? A purse probably flew out of your first diaper."

He rolled his eyes. "Well, not *you*, per se…your mother. She says your mom and your grandmother make bad magic and it rubbed off on me. She thinks bad magic turned me gay. Can you believe that crap? As if anything but

3

Divine Providence and Twenty-first Century Fabulousness had any influence on this. In her own warped way I guess she's trying to rationalize it. The dummy means well."

"Everyone has a redeeming quality, I guess. But your parents don't have to blame something you were born with on us. My mom's been really good to your mom. When she was alive, my grandmother loved your mom. She used to help her all the time. I remember your mom would always get my granny to read her cards and give her remedies for her stomach. It's shitty of her to think so poorly of us. Not all magic is evil, but being judgmental definitely is."

Benny shrugged. "What can I say? This place is full of uneducated Catholics."

Astrid was about to say something when he swished his hands at her. "Hey, totally random but did you notice the snakeskin in the corner of the cemetery, near the entrance? By the trash can?" he picked at the corner of his nail beds.

"Snakeskin? No. I didn't see anything. You would have heard me shrieking. Aren't they supposed to be hibernating?"

"Astrid, we're in South Texas," he spat a piece of skin to the ground. "We don't have a winter. But you're right. They don't usually come out around this time. But I thought this was cool and interesting. There was also an empty duffel bag thrown by the side of a grave. I bet is had money or drugs. You know the cartels use the cemetery to smuggle things—at least that's what my dad says. I checked inside but it was empty. I did find this though." He pulled something out of his pockets.

For a moment, she couldn't quite tell what the object was and carefully picked up the strange interlocking segments. Astrid let it drop when she realized it was part of a rattlesnake's tail.

"Don't drop it, dumb-dumb. It's good luck."

"Benny, that's a snake rattler!" Astrid shook her small, thin frame. "Get it away from me!"

"I know. I found it with the snakeskin. I pulled it off."

"Why would you give that to me, you know I'm terrified of snakes. And why is it that color?"

"I don't know. I've never seen snakeskin this color. Blue. I thought it was pretty. Like my hair. Maybe it can be a lucky charm. Lord knows you need luck," he said, carefully cleaning off pieces of dirt.

"I don't want it. Snakes give me the creeps."

"It's not going to hurt you. Don't give power to things you fear. It's good to have things that scare you around. It lets the universe know you can handle anything it throws at you. Let the universe know you're brave."

She sighed and reluctantly accepted the rattler. "I've always wanted to be braver."

"And so it is," smiled Benny.

Astrid held the rattler in her hand then shook it near her ears before placing it inside her jean jacket pocket. A short distance away from the pair, coiled beneath pieces of rotting tree branches, a blue-colored rattlesnake raised its flat head, stuck its black forked tongue out and quietly slithered behind them.

Carnelian Red

T HE TINY ROOM at the back of the Cortez home wasn't ready for visitors. Sarah rarely even allowed her daughter, Astrid, to enter the room containing their family altar. But how could she say no to an old, family friend like Luci? When she begged for a card reading, the pain in Luci's voice compelled Sarah to agree. "My daughter is in trouble again," cried Luci in Spanish. The trembling voice shattered Sarah's heart. "Ruby's headaches are back. And they are worse than ever before. I need a reading."

"Come over now," said Sarah. "Astrid is not here. I don't want her to know I'm doing readings again. Try to hurry."

Luci eagerly replied, *"Voy en camino.* I'm on the way." This allowed Sarah enough time to put on some jeans, comb through her curly, black hair, and make her way to the small altar room.

Sarah hadn't read anyone's cards in over three months and couldn't quite remember where she had left her Corodona set, the special tarot cards only made in Spain. They were a beautiful deck with intricate designs her sister, Marianne, gave her years earlier. Those were her favorite. She rummaged through the shelves on the back wall, looking through the endless crates and boxes. "Stop hiding."

After lighting a candle and setting an intention to cleanse the room of stagnant energy, Sarah took a deep breath. "I'm sorry," she whispered towards the shelves. "I'm sorry. But I need you now." Her eyes instinctively closed and she turned toward the left side of the altar. Her fingers guided her towards a red box with a painted white crown and several *milagros* nailed to it. "There you are." Taking out the silk-wrapped tarot deck, Sarah tried not to stare at the strange, little plastic doll resting with the cards. The faded toy emitted a putrid odor. The barbed wire bounding it was beginning to rust. It looked angry—a carnelian red. "Again with the resistance. I'll fix you later," she told the doll.

At that moment, Sarah heard a rapping at the screen door. Framed in the doorway was Luci's petite and frail silhouette. Her shadow carried heavy, dark energy. "Thank you for seeing me," Luci said before entering the altar room.

They sat at a flimsy, aluminum poker table covered with a *rebozo*, a Spanish shawl. Sarah did not want to notice the dark circles around Luci's typically bright eyes or the paleness in her friend's normally caramel skin. Luci averted eye contact as Sarah shuffled the deck of cards.

"It has such beautiful colors," Luci forced a smile while running her fingers over the shawl's aged embroidered flowers. She drew back her hands when Sarah placed the deck in front of her.

"This was my grandmother's. I found it in a drawer the last time I went to her house. It was in a cabinet, covered in dirt and webs. I'm surprised no one took it. Astrid and I are going back tomorrow. I want to see the inside one last time. Astrid wants to take pictures for her class. You know how she is with that camera."

"When are they going to tear down the house?"

"The government said they were going to tear it down in April, but who can say?"

Sarah handed the tarot cards to Luci. "But to the point—shuffle. It's the same as always, shuffle them three times. Think about a question you want answered."

Luci sat up straight. "*Dios nos libre.* God help us."

"*Tranquila*, Luci. Everything is going to be alright."

Sarah inspected the frailty in Luci's hands. She was thinner now, and even though they were both in their early forties, Luci looked considerably older. Frown lines dominated her face, branding both sadness and dissolution.

Luci set the cards down. "I saw her crying yesterday." Luci wiped away her tears. "It's terrible seeing your baby cry. It breaks you."

"You're a good mother. A good person. *No llores*—don't cry, Luci."

"Am I?" she shrugged. "I used to drink a little before I knew I was pregnant," she leaned in and whispered. "Is that what caused this?" Luci's eyes widened.

Sarah shook her head. "I don't know."

"Can you find out?" She nudged at the cards. "Can they tell you things like that?"

"This isn't a medical exam, Luci. I only repeat what they tell me."

"I want them to tell me why Ruby gets so dizzy. Why can't she step outside into the sun without her eyes burning?"

"Have you taken her to the doctor?"

"No," she scoffed and shrugged her shoulders. "With what insurance?"

"Doesn't she qualify for CHIPS or some other program? Medicaid?"

Luci sighed.,"*Pues que te digo, Sarah, me pendejie.* I screwed up."

"What do you mean?"

"I went to visit my mother before I gave birth to Ruby. I didn't make it back in time, and I ended up having her in Mexico."

"And you never got her Naturalization papers in order?"

"I barely got mine fixed, let alone hers. I can't afford a lawyer. So many years living in this country for nothing."

Luci placed her black purse on her table, unzipped it, and removed a handkerchief. She blew her nose and kept her eyes fixed on the bag momentarily. Her gaze was broken by Sarah's voice.

"Luci, you've been working for the Felton's for years. How did you work with them if you didn't have papers? George is a police officer. Did they know?"

"They knew," she raised her eyebrows. Her look said, "They knew very well what was going on. But now that they have the *Migra*, that damned Border Patrol, here all the time he helped me take care of my Immigration status. Mr. Felton has an uncle who works in Washington. *La Señora* Regina helps me raise money to pay for the doctor's visits by letting me have Bingos at *La Rosa*. They are good people. She even provides the prizes. They are fake bags but they are still nice. No one can tell they aren't real." Luci put the handkerchief back in her purse and sighed.

"And with all the Border Patrol agents in the area? Weren't you afraid of getting caught?"

Luci shrugged her shoulders. "Every day. But what could I do? I need to work."

The two women sat in silence for a moment until Luci twisted her lips to the side and said, "You won't get mad at me?"

"About?"

"I don't think I can go on with the card reading. I changed my mind. *No se,* a part of me doesn't want to know what's going on. Perhaps it's better not to know the future? Let it be God's will."

"No, why would I get mad?"

"Maybe I needed to vent. Maybe I just needed to talk to someone." She stood up. "I feel silly now," she covered her face. "I'd better go before your Astrid gets back."

Sarah stood up too. "Take care of yourself when you get home. Now I'm worried about you being pulled over. This government changes rules all the time."

"I think the Border Patrol only pulls over people they don't recognize, but they see me all the time. Mr. Felton talked to them so they wouldn't stop me before I got my green card. I think he knows someone who told them not to bother me. I think he is friends with important people."

"Probably," she agreed. "The Felton's do know a lot of people. But still, be careful."

"The things we do for our children," she smiled weakly, then hugged Sarah, giving her a kiss on the left cheek. "The things we do for love."

Sarah fixed her gaze on a red box that held her tarot cards. "The things we do for love."

"Listen, I know I changed my mind, but I have a friend who is having trouble with her man. Do you think you could read her cards?"

"I'm not really reading anymore. I only said yes to you because you really needed my help. I never say no to a friend."

"She needs your help, too. *Andale.* She's in a bad place."

Sarah hesitated at first but then said, "Have her call me. I just don't need

Astrid to find out I'm doing readings. She worries about me."

"It's been so long since I've seen Astrid. She doesn't go to the Felton's anymore."

"No. Astrid's in her room all day or taking pictures. She lives with that camera around her neck. But she's still friends with Benny. I haven't seen him in ages either."

"That kid is crazy! The things he says! And Does!" Luci chuckled. "He has soft blood, so easygoing and agreeable. I don't judge him like others do. We're no one to judge people."

"Well, I'm sure his mother certainly does."

"What can I say," sighed Luci, "She wants him to have a good life. She loves him a lot. She's not the kind of woman to show it, but she does. I know it. I see it."

"She sure has a messed up way of showing it. I've heard the way she speaks to him. And he's told me some stories about her. I think that's why he did what he did last year. He's sensitive. She needs to be careful about what she tells him or next time we won't be so lucky."

"I know, but what can I say. He's not my kid. But every mother does what she can. What wouldn't I do for my kid? What would any of us not do for our children?" She was quiet for a moment and then asked, "Are you going to the cemetery with your sisters this week?"

Sarah raised her eyebrow inquisitively. "How did you know?"

"I overheard your sister Julia telling *La Señora* Regina the other day."

"I didn't realize they were still friends after all these years."

Luci scoffed. "*Son uña y carne.* They are one and the same."

"Makes sense. They're both terrible people."

Luci pressed her lips together for a moment before saying, "*Bueno*, I should go." She rose from her seat. "How much do I owe you?"

"What do you mean, I didn't do anything?" she exclaimed.

"*Gracias.* The little talk helped." Luci sighed. "Please be careful when you go later this week. I heard there were snakes in the cemetery."

"We're in the middle of winter. They don't come out now."

"Still," Luci insisted. "Be very careful. My husband told me he found snakeskin when he was cleaning there earlier this morning."

Sarah touched the side of Luci's shoulder. "I'll be careful. Come and visit me more often."

"I will. But you should be aware that some snakes *do* come out in winter."

Sarah cocked her head to the side, unsure how to respond.

Luci looked on sympathetically and gently grasped at Sarah's hands. "And they're closer than you think."

Nocturnal Kingdom

ASTRID PLACED THE blue rattle Benny gave her earlier in a mason jar on her desk. She stared at the object for a moment, before remembering an essay she needed to complete for her Yearbook class. It took her about two hours to finish, but it probably would have been quicker if she hadn't stopped to look at a bunch of TikToks Benny kept sending her. When she received the last text, "Girl……This is the kind of cat I want…. Buy me one… Benny Like. Benny Like… Quit being a Rhymes With Runt and Replyyyyy!!!" She ended up turning off her phone and submitted the assignment just before midnight.

Astrid always had an easy time falling asleep. She never understood why Benny had such trouble in that department. It amazed her how he was able to stay awake most nights and function normally with three or four hours of sleep.

"You know Benny," she remembered asking him once. "I've always wondered how someone with so few thoughts could end up staying up so late? You even call yourself a dumb bitch all the time. Aren't you bored out of your mind?"

"I DO think," he snapped. "Just because I'm not all philosophical doesn't mean I don't think. I have dreams, you know. I stay up thinking about how I'm going to make my millions."

"You come from money. What do you need millions for?"

"Nah, girl," said Benny. "Don't you know old money doesn't last. Just because we live in a nice house doesn't mean we're loaded. Look at where we live, dude. You think we'd have stayed here if we had real money? We would have sold all our land like my aunt Claire did and moved away after her husband left her."

"Everyone thinks you're rich, dude. Your house has a name for God's sake."

"Everyone also thinks my mom's nice and my dad's a decent human being, but we know better," he replied.

"It's easy for me to sleep. I just rest my head then boom—dead to the world. It's like I leave my body for eight hours."

"You're lucky. It takes me a good hour," Benny bemoaned, "But it would probably be less if I wasn't on my phone. I just hate that I have such vivid dreams."

Astrid hesitated momentarily. "Can you remember your dreams?"

"Yeah. I remember all of them. It's like I'm watching a movie. But they are always weird. Like once I dreamt huge bears were floating on the river. And another time I dreamt I was on this unfinished highway and giant tigers were staring at me."

"Jesus."

"Yeah, that one freaked me out. Don't you have any nightmares?"

"No," said Astrid. "Honestly, I don't remember any of my dreams. I don't even know if I actually have any."

"That's weird, dude. Everybody dreams."

She shrugged her shoulders. "I guess I'm just not a dreamer."

But this night would be very different. As she lay in bed, her eyes fixed on the rattle from earlier. *What kind of snake would have a blue rattler*, thought Astrid. *Blue stands out in nature. Blue wants to be seen.* This was something she had never heard of before.

Eventually though, Astrid's thoughts subsided. The strange sensation started at the crown of her head, as if static and stars were whirling around her, forming a cosmic crown that traveled throughout her body. Her core temperature dropped almost instantly. She should have been sinking into sleep, but a sense of wrongness permeated the air. Astrid initially felt tingling in her feet, almost unnoticeable at first, but as the sensation progressed up her calves towards her hip, she became aware of it. The feeling was like being swallowed whole, like a giant anaconda eating its prey. There was something different going on. She usually lost track of her thoughts at this point, but part of her was still very aware. She knew she was falling asleep (or was she already asleep?). While immobile, Astrid felt the receptors of her brain firing. The whirring of her inner machine was audible.

Astrid instantly became aware of every strand of hair on her body, of the cellular processes inside her, and of the separation of atoms within atoms. She could hear the microscopic language that spoke her into existence and feel everything that was building her body. Astrid let the stream of static wash over her subconscious and conscious mind. Suddenly, tingles danced across her skin as darkness swallowed her whole. Then, as if some unseen force had turned on a switch, she opened a new set of eyes, ones that floated over her sleeping body. Her eyes scanned her small bedroom like a bird perched atop a shelf. There was an air of life and vividness to the strange dream, as if it were more real than reality. Twinkling lights floated around the electrical outlets, and even her computer screen. It was as if she could see the energy in the machine pulse and flow.

The dream brought with it spectacular vision. Astrid was reminded of a report she had written about owls for a middle school biology class. She felt like a great owl hovering in her room. Her eyes, two great big cameras scanning the room in high definition. She remembered that the owls had the greatest eyesight in all of the animal kingdoms. In this new Nocturnal Kingdom, Astrid was the greatest owl, with powerful and precise focus even in the dimly lit room.

Her vision drifted higher as she panned up into the small attic above her room. Dust and cobwebs lined the unfinished areas of the small space. She could see the night's blue light from an air duct on the north side of the room and made her way towards it. Astrid floated out and could now see the midnight moon. The dream made the orb's glow even more radiant. A spinning light twirled around the moon in a hypnotic rhythm. She had never seen anything more beautiful.

Then an unexpected coldness took hold of her. A movement in the grass caught her attention as she looked down towards the ground. While floating down, she noticed a snake slithering toward her house. Something was very different about this animal though. Astrid had seen real snakes before, during

14

summer it was almost impossible not to see a rattlesnake or a coral snake slithering across the road. But this creature was distinctly unusual. It emitted a strange glow and stopped slithering the moment it realized Astrid was staring down at it.

It raised its head and fixed its attention on the sky, scanning the area and flicking its tongue as if smelling for something. Eventually, it lowered its head and continued slithering towards the small room at the back of Astrid's home, to her mother's altar room. Astrid was about to follow the snake when she caught sight of another snake staring at her from a tree. This one wasn't flicking its tongue. It was coiled on a branch and angrily hissed at her. It's rattle began shaking violently. The sounds made her spirit tremble.

In an instant, Astrid felt herself transported back into reality and her eyes shot open. She found herself in a haze, struggling to shake off the nightmare—was it a nightmare?—as a cold sweat clung to her like a second skin. While she lay in bed, her mind wavered between what was real and what was just a product of her subconscious. In her groggy state, she reached for her phone to check the time but caught sight of the blue rattle in the mason jar. For a moment, she swore she could hear it rattling.

Talavera Road

SARAH AGREED TO drive Astrid to her grandmother's house on Talavera Road on Sunday. Astrid had been bugging her all week about taking her to the abandoned home to take photos for her "Beauty in Decay" project. The dreary morning brought light drizzle as they drove down the sleepy, winding roads. Camera in hand, Astrid would ask her mother to stop the car periodically as she photographed the various homes in Diller. While some homes were kept neatly, manicured with wooden fences and gardens, others were enclosed by chain-link fences. In Diller, there were those who prospered and those who gave up; it was a town of extremes. Usually, those who prospered chose to leave.

Astrid snapped a photo of an abandoned lot with both overgrown patches of grass and cracked, dry earth. *Prosperity for some, desolation for others.* That was a visual representation of the town of Diller. Case in point, thought Astrid, as she stared at Benny's majestic family residence, *La Rosa.* At the corner of Ramiro Baez and Main Street, the two-story structure had always been Astrid's favorite. It was an old Victorian-style house–a great dollhouse built by Benny's grandfather as a gift to his first wife. At one point, the shiplap exterior had a pinkish hue, but Regina Felton had since painted it white. There was nothing like it in any of the South Texas ranch land. It was a jewel among rocks.

The five remaining houses on Talavera Road were abandoned after the government declared their properties would be purchased through eminent domain laws. The government had decided to construct a section of a border wall behind their homes but never actually started on that section of the project. Following the delivery of the official documents, Sarah's sister Sofia spearheaded efforts to get all the sisters to sign and notarize the necessary legal documents. Each of the four daughters received a measly 600 dollars in the end. The houses at the end of the road were about to be bulldozed. Sarah and Astrid parked by the side of the road then walked towards the gray brick structure that remained. They surveyed the perimeter before entering the small, dilapidated structure that was once Sarah's grandmother's home.

"Jeez, I think our living room is bigger than the whole house," said Astrid.

"They were poor, Astrid. Were you expecting Versailles? Buckingham Palace?"

"Well no," she explained, "But how am I going to find interesting things here? I need to take like 40 photos."

"I don't know why you're acting so surprised. You know your aunts took most of the furniture from inside. You've been here before."

"I thought this place was bigger, with more to see."

"Well, we can always take pictures of the river. It's behind that little shed."

"I guess," she shrugged. "That might be interesting."

"Can you imagine?" said Sarah. "Having to pee in there."

"Where?"

Sarah turned Astrid towards a run down structure several yards from the house. "That little shed. It's an 'outhouse.'"

"No way." Snap.

"They didn't have plumbing back then. You had to go in there. That's why grandma used to say 'voy pa' fuera,' when she needed to go to the bathroom. They literally had to go outside to do their business."

"Seriously? Tell me they at least had toilet paper."

"Oh my God. Of course there was, but imagine during the winter. Like today? Imagine having to go all the way out there just to pee. Or running out at night during a storm. Imagine you get *choro* from eating bad food. You'd have to use the bathroom with all the worms crawling inside the hole in the ground," she cringed. "You don't know how lucky you are."

"How lucky WE are… You work in a Library mom. The most you struggle with is a paper cut. You wouldn't survive very long roughing it in the wild ranch lands of South Texas."

"Paper cuts and budget cuts," she joked. "You'd be surprised what I can do. If I can survive a sarcastic daughter like Astrid Cortez, I can handle anything."

"Hardy-har, mom." She snapped a photo of the structure then inspected it. "Meh, I can use it for something, I guess."

"It's funny. I never paid any attention to this house until now. Never knew I cared about it until I found out that the federal government was going to bulldoze it to the ground."

Astrid scanned the property with her camera. "Beauty in the Decay. There's something beautiful in its dreariness. I'm sure a lot of good things happened here."

Sarah raised her eyebrows. "A lot of bad things, too."

"Mom, you're such a pessimist."

"And you're full of toxic positivity."

"It's not toxic to have hope," affirmed Astrid.

"It is when you have hope of turning this dump into a showroom. There's nothing beautiful about this. They were very poor, Astrid. That's the reality. Why are you trying to sugarcoat their misery?"

"I'm not trying to sugarcoat it. If you don't like the house so much, why did you bring me?"

"I came because you said you had this project to do. It just makes me feel weird that you find beauty in this. A lot of suffering happened here."

To lighten the mood, Astrid lowered her voice, held the camera against her face and pretended it was a TV cameraman. "Ms. Cortez, what is your fondest memory of this place?"

"Oh, so now you're a journalist, too?"

"I'm asking the questions here, Lady. I repeat, what is your fondest memory here? Come on, even Eli Wiesel had some uplifting stories about the camps, Ma'am."

Sarah inspected the interior of the home. "There's mold on the ceiling. We shouldn't breathe it in."

"Deflect much? Answer the question, Sarah Cortez."

"I don't know," she shrugged. "I didn't visit this place very often. This place has bad energy. Just take your photos so we can go." She put her hands in her pocket, then found herself lost in thought.

"Ms. Cortez," said Astrid. "The video is still running. And remember, the camera adds ten pounds. Twenty on you."

Sarah smiled as a thought formed in her mind's eye. "God, you're a pest. Fine," she lifted her hands in defeat. "I remember once when we were here visiting. Grandma Agustina–that's grandma Carmen's mother–she was very short, tiny. She looked like an old girl, if that makes sense, barelt five feet tall. I think I was taller than her when I was 10. She always wore her little shawl, even when it was hot. She would always scare me and my sister, Marianne, with her stories. I used to love hearing her *cuentos*. She said she would fly at night."

"Did the Pinched Sisters ever visit here?"

"The Pinched Sisters?" Sarah repeated.

"Yes, your sisters. That's what I call Aunt Sofia and Aunt Julia? I call them that because their faces always looked like they were eating lemons. They always have their lips tightly puckered in anger. Like a mean little butthole."

"You're so bad," Sarah laughed. "No. They were older than me and married. But my other sister Marianne and I would come here a lot. One time grandma Agustina told us a story about how she used to speak to the wind."

"Like the *actual* wind? Psychotic much?"

"Don't mock her. She said she would ride the wind. That she would fly at night. She would travel all over. Back to her home in Mexico and visit her family. Grandma said our family were Those Who Ride the Wind. She was old and I was young. I liked hearing about the places she supposedly visited. One day, while she was telling us a story, the wind started to pick up speed. Then all of a sudden, Marianne's hair began to whirl and spin. Her hair looked like it had snakes screaming at the sky."

"Are you serious?"

"You come from a long line of witches, Astrid. Don't you know there's magic in Cortez women?"

She lowered her camera as a small crease appeared between her eyebrows."I don't have any gifts. I can't read the cards like you. I'm not a healer like grandma. I don't ride the wind like great-grandma Agustina. The most magical thing in my life is a disgruntled fairy named Benny."

Sarah burst into laughter. "Oh, *mija*, believe it or not, not having magic can be a gift all its own."

The Fourth Gorgon Sister

MORNINGS AT *LA ROSA* were always quiet. A typical morning for Regina Felton involved checking social media, waiting for Luci to prepare breakfast and watching the birds outside her kitchen window. She liked the cardinals the most. Their red color stood out against the beige backdrop of South Texas. However, as the sun rose that morning, there was no movement, just a heavy weight of a mild Texas winter.

"There's nothing worse than waking up from a pleasant dream, Luci," she told her housekeeper in a dry, low voice. "I had a good one last night. A strange but pleasant dream. I wasn't afraid, and I wasn't nervous about anything."

"What was the dream about?" Luci spoke in Spanish and Regina spoke in English. Before pulling out a chair and sitting at the table with Regina, Luci wiped her hands on her floral apron.

"I was sewing something I wasn't using traditional materials like cotton or polyester though. It was liquid-like, but worked like fabric. It looked like the midnight sky. A few areas were brighter than the others, with stars and constellations. The scissors were golden, and I was cutting and cutting away. I would pin the cloth onto a mannequin."

"Were you making a dress?"

Regina pursed her thin lips to the side. "I don't think so. I think I was making a shirt for Benny. I kept thinking about him while I was dreaming."

"Can you think in a dream?"

"I think so. I was dreaming that I was thinking of Benny while I made the outfit. And it makes sense because the other day he demanded I buy him a shirt with stars on it. He got upset when I told him no. I guess it stayed in my

21

mind."

"So that was the dream? You were sewing for him?"

"Well, yes," said Regina. "But that's not the best part. That's not why I was upset when the dream ended. While I was sewing the shirt, I realized that the material was flexible but very strong. It was like liquid armor. I think the fabric was made out of the night. I think it's meant to be worn to hide, to conceal, to walk behind the night. The shirt makes you invisible. Protects you from evil eyes. And we all know there are many evil eyes around here."

"You were creating armor for Benny."

"Oh yes!" she exclaimed with pride. "I felt pleased knowing I could protect him."

"Then why do you look so *callida*, so down? That was a good dream."

"Because it was only a dream, Luci. Reality melts the dream." She sipped her coffee, cleared her throat then abruptly changed the topic. "When you went and talked to Sarah yesterday, did you find out if Sarah was going to be at the cemetery with Julia and Sofia? She doesn't reply to their texts."

"Yes. Sarah told me she was going."

"Good. The Cortezes are such a broken family. I want to make sure they find peace."

"Why don't you invite them here, to *La Rosa*?"

Regina scoffed, dismissing the suggestion. "I didn't think Sarah would come here."

"Why?"

"She doesn't like me. I mean she'll talk to me if I see her in public, but I know she doesn't care for me. Sarah used to date George several years ago." A wicked smirk formed across Regina's pale face.

Luci widened her eyes. "Sarah and Mr. Felton?"

Regina slowly nodded her head. "Yes. But he ended up marrying me. That's what matters."

"Ah. I see. She never told me."

"She's not going to tell you. After all, George ended up with the best, didn't he?" Regina smirked. "Besides, I don't want Benny spending time with Astrid. I don't want her to take advantage of my Benny."

"Advantage?"

"Well, yes. I know what girls her age are after."

Luci furrowed her eyebrows. "Astrid? But they are just friends."

"I was just friends with George. Look what happened to us."

"That shouldn't be a problem," she half-laughed.

"Why," Regina's voice suddenly turned sour. "Why wouldn't it be a problem? My Benny is a very handsome young man."

"But he's…" her voice drifted. "He sees her as a friend," she struggled to find the right words.

"Yes. And Astrid is very pretty. I don't want him ruining his future by having an accident."

"No. No, you're right. He needs to be careful." Part of Luci wanted to laugh. The other part wanted to keep her paycheck.

"Girls at her age are dangerous. They see an innocent boy and try to take advantage of him. And then if they have a little bit of money. *Callate*. She'll destroy him."

"You're right, *Señora*."

Luci had to bite her tongue to keep from laughing. By the end of the conversation, she tasted blood. "I know you love Benny very much."

"Tell him that for me, will you? He thinks I'm a monster. He called me The Fourth Gorgon Sister the other day. Just because I didn't let him use his car."

"What does that mean?"

Regina hands were raised dismissively. "*Cosas de Benny*. I have no idea, but I can't imagine it's a good thing."

"That Benny is something else."

She nodded. "Yes. And one day his mouth will get him into a lot of trouble."

"But he has you to support him. You and your husband."

"Yes, he has us. But it won't do him any good when he leaves. He'll have no one protecting him while he's away. I worry about him going to college. What use is a name if no one knows it? But I will give him the armor he needs. That will–" Regina's voice trailed off, and she suddenly stopped speaking. She was frozen momentarily by an unseen force. Her bright eyes turned dim and red. Luci had never seen sadness take hold of someone so quickly.

Taking a deep breath, Regina lifted her head and closed her eyes. Luci could tell Regina was fighting back tears. "Luci, I don't understand why you humor me. After all these years I think of you as a friend. It is not necessary for you to patronize me. It's what you think I want, but I don't. Not really. I am very aware of what people say about my Benny. That's why he needs this armor. That's why I'm going to do what I need to do."

"What are you going to do?"

"I've been thinking a lot about it," Regina stared into Luci's eyes. "I think it's for the best. I'm going to take him to visit someone who can protect him. I'm going to help my Benny walk behind the night. Make him go unnoticed."

"Making Benny invisible is almost impossible. He stands out. Benny is Benny."

"It's not his fault he stands out," Regina lifted her head high. "That's why I don't want him associating with Astrid. Or her mother. That's why I don't let him go over to their house anymore. I think her family did something to him. He never used to act like this before."

"Did what?"

Regina turned to Luci with wide eyes. "You know."

Luci looked away.

"You know what I mean, Luci. I know everyone thinks it."

"I don't judge. I'm not God."

"But others will," Regina sighed. "I don't know what else to do. But these people said they could cure him. I must do whatever it takes to save my boy."

"Any mother would," said Luci.

"Yes," tears formed in the corners of her eye. "A good mother would."

Residual Magic

LAUREL HIGH SCHOOL was dead. By four o'clock that Monday, the small, rural high school had emptied of nearly all its eight hundred students. A few hours earlier, two girls, Stephanie and Yamilex, had fought in the middle of University Hall, the building's main artery. So much hair had been pulled off that they could have made a wig prop for the drama kids.

Astrid pointed at a water fountain. "Look-look-look! That's where the fight started," she said.

Benny rolled his eyes aggressively. "I'm glad they beat the crap out of Yamilex. I can't stand that chick. She never lets me borrow her English homework. Too bad William Shakespeare couldn't save her from the beat down she got. *Fair is foul, and foul is fair.* She got what she deserves," he cackled.

"Benny, you hate everyone."

"I don't hate *you.*"

Astrid laughed to herself. "You're so dumb. What did you all do in Kidder's class?"

"Were you skipping? Why didn't you text me!"

"No. I was at a presentation for St. Michael's University. I didn't want to do another one of those career surveys," she said. "I never know what to check off in those occupation questionnaire surveys the counselors keep giving us. I mean, I like taking pictures, so does that mean I want to be a photographer? Or is it something I tell myself so people can help identify me? Oh, there's the girl with the camera. She must be artsy. I like my camera, and I'm OK at taking photos, but does it make me wake up in the morning? Does it make me want to achieve some unattainable goal so people (and I) realize I have a purpose? That I'm not wasting my supposed talent."

"Girl, we're like sixteen. No one expects anything from us."

"Yeah, they do, Benny. Expectations are caked on us. Go to college, pick a career at seventeen, don't marry till your ovaries are raisins. Make sure you are nice and smile. Land a decent looking, wealthy man so your kids don't suffer in the future."

Benny nodded, "Deep shizz."

"WE'RE in deep shizz," she emphasized.

"For reals. I can't decide on my future either. I can't even decide what hair color looks best on me."

"Growing up sucks balls, Benny," said Astrid.

"Yup," he agreed, "and not even pretty ones. Oh, before I forget, I didn't tell you about my encounter with Coffee House Hunk yesterday, did I?"

"No," replied Astrid. "Did you finally work up the courage to make eye contact?"

"Even better!" Benny's eyes widened with glee.

"Tell me."

"Well, my dad wanted me to drop off some papers at my Uncle's house in Norton City. Afterward, I drove to CuppaCuppa's for an iced coffee. I was hoping he was there and he sure as shizz was! When I got to the window to pay, our eyes met. They lingered. Like, I felt a surge—electric almost. I know he felt it as well because he smiled. Smiled! Then I was all like, "Can I have some extra sugar?" I didn't even need any, I'm watching my calories this week, but I wanted to keep the conversation going. Girl! Guess what he did when he came back?"

"Gave you the sugar?" she said blankly.

"Better," he beamed. "He shook the sugar?"

Astrid stared at Benny for a moment, trying to process the sentence. "OK. I give up. I have no idea what you're talking about."

"You know," he said, "He shook the packages before he gave them to me."

It took a while for her to register the statement, but eventually: "Oh, he shook them to level them off for you?"

"YES!" Benny squealed. "It's genuinely the most romantic thing anyone has ever done for me! He took the time to shake it. He took the time to shake it FOR ME!"

Astrid's jaw dropped. "Are you serious? That's your big news! What if he has Parkinson's and shakes everyone's sugar?"

"Why do you always have to go there?" scoffed Benny. "I mean, it was a sweet gesture. He didn't have to shake my sugar. He did it out of love."

"Well, if that's not pure love, I don't know what is."

"Uhh. I knew you would ruin it for me—typical Astrid. I had a moment, and you couldn't wait to burst it. Coffee House Hunk and I had a moment, which is more than I can say for you and Dylan Arias."

"Shut your hole, Benny." She lowered her head and looked around the empty hallway. "Whatever, at least I'm not getting my panties in a knot over some sugar packages like you are."

"Oh, please. I see the way you look at him. Trying to play it off like you don't stare at him every chance you get. At least I accept love. Do you hear this Universe? I. Accept. Love!"

She was quiet for a moment. "I accept love," she said with a tinge of resentment. "I just don't want to get my hopes up."

"Love is hope."

"I'm not in love, Benny!"

"Then what are you?"

She shrugged, "Desperately infatuated?" she let out a long sigh. "I can't help it, Dylan's so hot. I want to eat his face so bad."

"Jeez. Calm down Hispanical Lecter."

"You know what I mean."

Benny nodded intently. "You want him to shake your sugar?" he quipped.

She formed a wide smile and laughed. "Yeah… I want Dylan to shake my sugar."

"Girl, there's nothing wrong with that!"

"He's so… hot. Like a dirty blonde, white Jesus without the forsaken look, you know."

"Preach," said Benny.

"It's not even his personality. Benny, this is pure aesthetics. The dummy doesn't even know how hot he is. How can you walk around NOT knowing you're a freaking God? Dummy could probably walk on water and doesn't even know it. It's blasphemous."

"Oh, please," said Benny. "Have you seen Dylan's father? He's going to age like cheap leather in the Sahara."

"You're just jealous."

"Oh no, it's not in my nature. I'm too self-absorbed to be jealous. Besides, I know I got it going on."

"Delusion?"

"No, Hater.. Pizzazz. You can't bottle this and spray it on like cheap cologne. This is a birthright, right here."

"Why am I friends with you?" Astrid shook her head. "Listen, if you're free this afternoon, you should come to my house. I'll be taking pictures of a fire tonight."

"And I'm the weird one?"

"Yes. But this is going to be interesting," Astrid's face lit up. "They're burning the sugarcane."

"Oh, I heard those ridiculous FFA kids talking about the fire. They came to ask me if I knew anything about it. I was like, "I don't own those fields, go ask my dad... they're his."

"They've had signs posted for a while now. You literally drive past them every day. Your family owns them. How can you not be even remotely aware of this?"

He shrugged his shoulders. "I'm in Benny World," he said.

"Well, if you're willing to step out of Benny World for about an hour, tonight's the night."

"Benny will consider your semi-interesting invitation." He cleared his throat, "Just so you know, the FFA kids I overheard included Dylan. So yeah. Your hunky hunk of hunk will be there. Tuh-night."

"OK," she shrugged, pretending not to care.

"So don't forget to cake on some makeup and perfume. It's going to be a night to remember. Perhaps this fire will spark a little romance between a quiet spitfire, gay-friendly, classically misunderstood photography freak with a tall, blonde and supposedly handsome as the day is long FFA dumb-dumb." Benny's long fingers scanned Astrid up and down. "You're such a cliche."

She shook her head and playfully rolled her eyes. "You're one to talk," she snapped. "But you're right. Stranger things have happened."

"Hey, have you ever thought about asking your mom for help with this?"

"With what?" asked Astrid.

"Well, with Dylan Arias."

"What kind of help?"

"Gee, I don't know, maybe asking her to read your cards or to give you a little love potion?"

The question *had* crossed her mind. What's the point of having a tarot card reading mother if you're not going to get little perks out of it, right? She played the scenario in her head and saw herself awkwardly fumbling and dancing around the issue while her mother looked at her with annoyance and love. It was a stare she had perfected over time. "What's the point of knowing the future if it spoils the present?" Her mother, Sarah, would undoubtedly say.

To which Astrid would reply, "You're killing your sales pitch, mom. Customers don't like to hear the truth. They like to hear a story. That yarn you're spinning is depressing as hell."

"Well," she would undoubtedly say, "depressing or not, there should be some truth to advertising. I've never had a client tell me that knowing a catastrophe was coming their way brought a smile to their face."

"But they will at least be prepared," Astrid would argue.

"You're never going to be prepared for truly terrible news. Knowledge doesn't shield you from the pain. Usually, it makes it worse."

"Damn," she'd say. "Pop my balloon, why don't you?"

"I'm a card reader, not a therapist, Astrid. Do you want advice and comfort? I'll get you a counselor."

"What if I only want hope?"

"Oh, I can give you hope. I can give you love and listen to you if you need me to, but you want me to read your cards and give you hope at the same time. Unfortunately, that's something I can't do. The future doesn't sugarcoat things for you. The card reader won't, but your mom will. Let's not blur the line, little girl."

Astrid knew her mother didn't want to involve her in "that" world. She didn't even like it when she went into her altar room in the back of the house. Astrid was shocked that her mother allowed her to photograph her during one of her reading sessions a few weeks ago. *It must be the menopause,* she thought.

"My mom doesn't like doing that stuff for me."

"Why?"

"She just doesn't," Astrid said firmly.

"Well, my mom's been going to a new card reader in Norton City. Maybe I can ask her where it is and I can drive us."

"I don't think that's going to happen."

"Oh, come on," said Benny, "I can always get a lock of his hair. Or I can steal something from his gym locker, don't ask me how I know the combination."

"I don't want to force anyone to fall in love with me."

"It's how things are done around here. Aren't you the one always blabbing on and on about our culture and heritage? Well, forced love is our way of paying homage to tradition. Magical slavery is part of our heritage! How do you think my mom got my dad?"

"What? How do you know?"

"She told me," nodded Benny. "She was drinking one Saturday night and she flat out told me."

"Your mom's weird, dude."

"And my dad is so absent minded that it would be easy to put a spell on him. I wish I could put a spell on him. I think he's embarrassed of me.

"That's a horrible thing to say."

"Yeah, but it's true. It must be hard on him being a police chief and living up to those standards. Men are men and real men walk around with guns and authority. I'm sure he wishes I were a real guy. I don't walk around with a gun, I walk around with sarcasm and three inch heels."

"I'm sure he doesn't think that about you," said Astrid.

"No, he does. But if he does want me to act like a man and walk around with a gun it wouldn't be that hard. My dad never locks the safe he keeps them in. It's easy to get one. He probably wouldn't even know if one went missing." Benny sighed and half smiled. "It is what it is. See you at the fire. *Parting is such sweet sorrow.*"

Banter with the Xennial

ASTRID SPRITZED THE NEARLY-NEW bottle of upscale perfume her mother gifted her for Christmas onto her wrist. She wondered why girls at school were so obsessed with scent. Did it truly make them more appealing? Would Dylan notice? She wished for something to catch his eye. He seemed oblivious to her presence. For now, there was no spark. But maybe, just maybe, tonight would change that.

She looked into the full-length mirror in her bedroom. Astrid felt at ease in her faded jeans and yellow "I Call the Shots" Photography Club shirt. She knew she was attractive; her long black hair framed her delicate tan face and almond-shaped eyes. While impressing others with her attire was never a priority, now at sixteen without a romantic prospect, she wondered if this mindset had been beneficial.

Astrid pulled out a paper titled "Photography Composition Techniques" from her backpack and set it on her bedroom desk. Her desktop screen was always a mess. She found the folder titled "PIX" and scrolled through them. A beautiful black and white shot of last year's Spring play was perfect for "Lines," because the floorboards formed lines towards Benny. She renamed the photo "USE FOR LINESSSS." As she continued, she found a group of Dylan Arias pictures, and her heart started to flutter. She renamed one of the photos: "DADDDDY AF".

When had she first fallen for Dylan? What had kindled that affection? Astrid had been in Yearbook class with her favorite teacher, Ms. Bunny Rodriguez, for a few weeks when she began to appreciate him. She'd seen him around, but it was only after Ms. Bunny paired them for a project that she truly started noticing. Initially, being teamed with Dylan made her slightly self-conscious, but as the projects progressed, she began enjoying his company. She found herself laughing genuinely at their conversations. As the weeks passed, Astrid eagerly anticipated their paired assignments. Her growing crush was evident, and even Ms. Bunny seemed to see it.

Astrid blushed, remembering that Ms. Bunny had recently paired them. "This is all random, y'all," she said in an unusually high-pitched voice. "I mean, it's the computer, y'all. There was no collusion. Blame it on the Russians if it makes you sleep better."

Astrid hated and loved her teacher for playing matchmaker. She never thought she'd be the girl with a crush on the school heartthrob, but the heart wants what the heart wants. As Astrid scrolled through the endless angles of Dylan Aria's chiseled face, she knew her heart was persistent. Thank goodness she had a plan.

"It's going to work," she whispered. The distinct roar of fire trucks drew Astrid immediately to her bedroom window. Three older men, unfamiliar to her, were lounging under a massive ebony tree, each puffing on a cigarette. Several pickup trucks pulled into the fields, but none bore the distinctive silver sheen of Dylan's double cab. A gift from his father on his seventeenth birthday, it sported a black steel Louvered Headache cab rack. How on earth did Astrid Cortez know such specific truck details? Dylan had spent quite a while explaining its significance, and his plans to fit strobe lights to it in the future.

"I thought about customizing it, maybe with the welding teacher's help. I know how to weld. Well, I'm still learning, but I've got the basics. I was thinking of adding my name on the back, or maybe a deer. Or something that's 'me', like a Superman logo—or a deer. Did I mention the deer? I like hunting them with my dad." He added that the truck was "pretty plain" as it was, implying it needed some flair. Astrid wondered, for a brief moment, if he *really* meant she was too plain for him. She felt a pang, thinking she might need some 'enhancements' to fit into Dylan's world. Yet, Dylan wasn't one for double meanings; he was straightforward, a boy drawn to shiny things with no hidden motives. That simplicity was part of his allure for Astrid.

While she constantly questioned and yearned for more, he was captivated by surface beauty without the urge to question. Astrid envied that ease, wishing she could shine just as effortlessly.

Where is his tall silhouette, brown hair, and piercing eyes? *He better show up! Benny better not have been lying. The blabbermouth is always full of sketchy information. Would Dylan even notice the perfume? Or the mascara? Did I even put it on correctly? I never wear this crap. God, he better notice me, and the lipstick! I'm trying. I'm trying to stand out here.* Astrid sprayed the perfume on the crook of her arm again. "I'm tired of being all plain. I want to be seen. I want to be shiny."

Astrid lifted her SLR camera from her desk, letting it hang around her neck. "Battery. Check. Memory card. Check." She took a photo of her homework with her phone. "Homework. Check," she muttered, then made her way down the stairs.

She snapped a photo of her mother as soon as she reached the bottom of the staircase. A pink Tiffany lamp gave the room just enough light for Sarah to read. Sarah sat cross-legged on the right side of an old burgundy sofa, calmly bouncing her leg as she read a novel. Her grandmother's antique lamp's beams illuminated the green, rose-patterned living room wallpaper.

Sarah was an accessible beauty, not leading lady material but certainly a supporting, strong vixen whose feisty attitude easily wins over an audience. Her mother's husky voice was a stark contradiction to her thin, slender frame. Sarah raised a finger but never let her eyes leave the book. "Don't you dare post that picture, little girl."

"Don't worry, mom. I'll call it 'Documentary Photography' when I submit it. They expect to see people at their worst."

"Then you should probably take a selfie," Sarah whipped back.

Astrid admired herself in the gold-plated antique mirror by the stairway. "Hardy-har, Mom. Hardy-har," she replied before applying some lipstick she pulled out of her jacket. "I saw the fire trucks arriving. It's almost sundown. I need to take some shots before it gets too dark. The Golden Hour waits for no one. I think they're going to start burning the sugarcane soon."

Sarah shook her head. "Why do you like to photograph weird stuff?" she said as she flipped a page.

"We're in the buttcrack of Texas, Mom. Nothing else to do around here. I'm surrounded by fields and brush."

"We're also home to one of the biggest political stories of the century. You know they've already started building the wall on the Salazar property. Why don't you take a picture of that? Why would anyone want to watch sugar cane fields burn? This behavior is bizarre. Do you just enjoy being a social outcast? Do yourself a favor and read a book."

"It's for a grade. I need some good action shots. I'd rather be weird and take human interest photos than read sappy romance novels. I'm bored, not bitter."

"Just give it time," Sarah's eyebrows shot up as she smirked. "Hey, I need to tell you something before you leave."

"What?" she grunted.

"Your aunts and I are cleaning your grandma's tombstone tomorrow afternoon," Sarah flipped through her book. "I'm gonna need you to come with us. The little fence we made for mom keeps tipping over and people keep stealing the flowers I put around her grave."

"Who would steal flowers from a cemetery?" asked Astrid in annoyance.

"I want you to come with me to the cemetery so I don't feel awkward around your aunts. They keep bringing up the will. They want to sell the acres in Norton City, but I'm not signing any papers. Besides, we need all the sisters to sign and your aunt Marianne already said she wouldn't either."

"Why does Marianne need to sign? She's not even a part of the family. She hasn't shown her face in years."

"She's still a Cortez daughter and needs to sign all the legal documents because mom didn't have a will."

Astrid shrugged her shoulders before slipping on her favorite faded, denim jacket. "Fine. I'll take photos of the grave houses while I'm there. So it's not a wasted trip."

"Oh, one more thing," continued Sarah. "A woman named Julie is coming tomorrow. I've got to rush back here by eight. Remind me, in case your aunts start babbling away."

"I thought you weren't reading cards anymore. Why did you agree to read hers? Is she dying or something?"

"It's some woman who's going thought a divorce. I felt bad and I want to help her. It's something I just have to do. You don't understand. Life exists outside of that camera lens you always carry. You can't just be a silent bystander your whole life."

"I'm not a silent bystander. Why didn't you tell me about these readings?"

"I don't tell you a lot of things."

"Sheesh. Why can't people be comfortable alone? Nothing wrong with being by yourself. Divorced and single seems sensible in this day and age. Have you seen the economy, Mom?" She smirked at her own words. "My generation is pretty much in the toilet."

"Those are some bitter words for a sixteen-year-old. You sure you don't want to start reading one of my romance novels?"

"Well," Astrid quipped, "I learned from the best." She blew her mother an exaggerated kiss. "And no. Romance is the last thing I need right now. What Astrid Cortez needs to do right now is to watch some fields get their torch on and get an 'A' on this project."

"Oh, make sure to snap a few pictures of Dylan Arias, too? I bet you'd want to get some good action shots of him."

Astrid froze, her mouth agape. "Who?"

Sarah smirked, "How often do you wear the perfume I bought you? I can smell it all the way over here. And the lipstick?"

"Umm, I don't know what—"

"—You always like his photos on social media, Astrid. You like almost everything that boy posts. There's a reason you're going outside. There's a reason you're wearing lipstick. Hell, I'm surprised Benny's not here with a makeup brush and a magic wand ready to makeover his little Cinderella for the ball," she laughed. "Otherwise, you'd be in your room watching re-runs. Don't play that game with me; I know you're not as odd as you want to seem. You're hoping you see this boy. He's a fireman—looks kind of cute in his profile picture."

She crossed her arms. "Um... you're like forty."

"A young man and his fire hose," she smirked, raising her eyebrows. "There is absolutely nothing wrong with looking for a hose when there's a fire."

Astrid exhaled heavily. "Yeah, I'm gonna go now, but I'm going to have to do a major sweep of all my followers when I come home," she shook her head with mock indignation. "Don't spend too much time on those books, Mom. Plenty of men out in the world." She signaled toward the sugar fields across their home.

"Oh, for heaven's sake! Jesus, you are a pain. I'll be in my bedroom." Sarah picked up her book and made her way towards the staircase.

"Why do we have to go clean up the cemetery?" Astrid grunted and placed her hand on Sarah's shoulders. "I don't want to be around those people. Besides, I know when I kick it I won't care what my grave looks like. In fact, I don't want one. Throw me to the wind."

Sarah rolled her eyes as she walked passed her up the stairs, "You're so dramatic! You should join Benny in his theater class and drop the photography."

"You can blame that on my mother."

"Don't bite your tongue, Astrid," she replied from the top of the stairs. "You're exactly like your grandmother. She's the one who always had a comeback. She was the one with your wicked little tongue. You most definitely are sassy and sarcastic. Grandma's little rattlesnake," mocked Sarah. "It's what she called you."

"So what were you, her anaconda? At least I have the decency to warn my victims." Astrid grimaced from below.

"No," affirmed Sarah. "I'm a little viper. Very tiny, but very deadly," she shook her shoulders and puckered her lips. "You're the anaconda. I'd hate to see what happens to someone when you set your eyes on them."

All the Flowers in my Field

I T WAS A PERFECT NIGHT to set the fields on fire.

In the past, Astrid would watch the burning of the sugarcane fields from the safety of her bedroom. It fascinated her, the way the embers fluttered upwards, like tiny fireflies that both united and destroyed. In a mere ten to twenty minutes, what took weeks to grow was irrevocably annihilated. It was beautiful in its savagery and uniquely American in its efficiency. *It's mesmerizing*, she thought to herself, *something haunting but necessary.* She didn't like the sound though, the loud, angry crackling. The furious sound that came with a noxious odor.

She once asked a ranch worker about the reason for burning the sugarcane. He informed her that it made harvesting easier. "We like efficiency. It requires less manpower if we go this route. What happens is the fire strips the sugar cane of all the leaves and trash around it. You can't get to the good stuff without burning the outer leaves." Astrid thought his words were poetic. *Maybe I am just like a sugarcane,* she thought to herself. Astrid knew there was sweetness inside her, but she was surrounded by debris. Perhaps today's burning would reveal something Dylan Arias found appetizing.

Astrid walked past her house and found a shortcut past the nearby church grounds, towards the Felton Fields. The town's park-walkers were already in full force, making their rounds around the baseball field across St. Mary's with gossip on their lips and sticks in hand. A couple of stray dogs ran in front of Astrid as she cut past two elderly women talking about a Mexican soap opera they couldn't stop watching. "And the ending caught me off guard," said one woman in Spanish. "I never would have imagined it. The mother was the one who poisoned the daughter. The mother! Can you believe that? What times are we living in?"

"Not even children are sacred anymore."

"This is why the world is falling apart," replied the other woman. One of them wore rosewater perfume. The scent triggered a memory of her maternal grandmother, Carmen.

In the memory, the plump older woman was standing inside the Felton fields wearing a pink, floral house dress. A tall, white-haired man stood beside her. Astrid wondered why his beard was so yellow. Samuel Felton, Benny's Grandfather, was a lifelong friend of Astrid's grandmother. "Carmencita," he said in his slow, bourbon voice, "All the flowers in my field aren't half as beautiful as your voice." She replied in Spanish: "And all the flowers in these fields couldn't hide the stench of your crap." The two erupted in laughter. Astrid was seven and looked at the two older people in amazement. She loved walking along the edge of the fields. It gave her life.

When was the last time she dreamt about her grandmother? It pained her to answer the question. *It's been over nine years. That's how long ago she passed. Passed? The word sounds so sterile, didn't it? As if we're all cars on a long road driving along until one day we're out of sight. Just a flash. A flash of light on a black night. Is that what she was? Is that what we are? Flashes on a dark night. One flicker and we're gone. What a terrible thought.* Astrid used to think of her grandmother often. One cannot erase the memory of love, but to dream of someone is something altogether different. Her *abuelita*, Carmen, used to tell Astrid that the dead visit their loved ones in dreams. Sadly, her grandmother had not visited her in a long time.

It was difficult to remember. Astrid rarely even acknowledged the eight by ten photo of her late grandmother hanging in their living room. The photograph had become background noise. Years ago, she would have followed the lines around the old woman's face and imagined being able to touch her skin again. To be able to run her little fingers through the old woman's white hair and kiss her warm forehead before going to school. To hear her aged voice tell her to take care of herself in Spanish and that the Virgin Mary would surely accompany her on her way. To feel the years and smell the past. Now, Astrid's eyes scanned without purpose. She didn't want to forget. Had she forgotten? She didn't purposely push her grandmother out of her mind's eye. It was life, the avoidance of pain. Life has a way of burying our sorrows, the cold nature of self-preservation. But on this particular night, Astrid felt a chilly sadness while on the path leading to the Felton fields. The memories of countless walks she took with her old granny came rushing back. The stories, those enchanting stories her granny told so well. She missed the Spanish folktales and the *dichos*, the wise sayings of the past. A breeze suddenly picked up, and Astrid could almost smell the faintest scent of roses. She felt at home.

From a distance, Astrid could see all of Diller from where she stood, the whole of the old town peppered across the lower elevation of this otherwise hilly area. She remembered her grandmother telling her in Spanish, "We never walk alone in Diller." Astrid was only six years old at the time, but the memory vividly projected in her mind's eye. She loved listening to Carmen, her grandmother, tell stories about her own grandmother. Astrid's grandmother told stories about her great-grandmother. "My grandmother Leonora would fly at night-she would be your great-great grandmother," the old woman recounted in Spanish. "You may not believe me, but it's true. I lived it. I saw it." She pointed her olive-toned finger towards the sky. "Especially in the middle of summer. That's when Grandma Leonora would ride the wind and travel down to Mexico to visit her relatives during the summer Canicula. That's a powerful time." Astrid loved those stories. "It's a gift we have," she would say while braiding her hair. "Some people are bone-setters. Some people read teardrops. Some people stare into crystals. Everyone has a gift. They can't see it—some don't want to see it. What a pity that some people deny their divinity. Nothing sadder than turning your back on gifts from God."

"God gave them their gifts?" asked Astrid.

"Yes, child. Who else would be so wonderful as to share His power?"

"God can set bones?"

"*Si, mija.*"

"God can read cards?"

"God can do anything. God made you."

"Can you ride the wind, Grandma? Like your grandmother? Can you ride the wind, too?"

"No," she smiled and exhaled deeply. Astrid loved her scent. "It's something I always wanted, but God didn't think it wise." Grandma Carmen squeezed Astrid's hands, "But he was generous with you."

"With me?"

"Si, *mija*. God has blessed you eternally."

"Eternally?"

Carmen nodded. "You have my grandmother's gift. You have something more special than anyone else on this planet. You have the greatest gift of all," she paused, then kissed Astrid's forehead. "You are not bound to your skin."

Astrid missed the stories. The majority of them didn't make sense to her, but she loved to listen to her grandmother's words. But all of that was in the past, the stories were gone. Almost overnight, the life she knew, the words and magic she knew had been easily replaced by the mundane, suburban bleakness of the everyday. She was pleased the walk triggered the memory. It sprang back so suddenly, as if the life inside an egg realized something waited for it outside of its shell. It scratched the inside until it made a crack, then, with a little more force, made a hole on the surface. Something was awake now. Something was here in Diller.

. "You are not bound to your skin," Astrid mumbled quietly to herself, then half-smiled. "What did that even mean?" She knew the answer. It was there, and she was waiting for its meaning to surface.

Her phone vibrated, jolting her back to reality.

BENNIE BFF:

Heyyyyyy

ASTRID:

Where are you?

BENNIE BFF:

Mars, Hoe…..

ASTRID:
It's going to be hot like Mars in a few.
Where are you?

BENNIE BFF:
Still at my house. 5 min.
Mom being a munch.

ASTRID:
K.
Hurry.
Just got here. Don't see him.

BENNY BFF:
Sorry, hoe.

The Latina Joan of Arc

"I NEED A FRAME within a frame," she said to herself. "Crap. I should have snapped a photo from the window before I got here. Skip." She continued down the list. "Juxtaposition. Juxtaposition. Hmm." She scanned the Felton Fields through the lens, zooming in on several faces hoping to find Dylan pulling up in his pick-up truck. No luck. "I'm such a stalker," she mumbled to herself before lowering the lens. She dropped her head dramatically. "This is so pathetic."

"I'm here," cried a voice from behind. Astrid's head jolted up.

Her friend sashayed before her. "Benny," she squeaked. "Where's your camera?"

"I couldn't unscrew it from the tripod. I was having a massive selfie session last night. I couldn't find my dad to help me take it off."

Benny's blue hair appeared luminous even in the dimming light. His pale skin glowed, but it could have just been the highlighter makeup. He was wearing skinny jeans and a red flannel top, a yellow bow tie, and black army boots. Benny was taller than her, especially since he insisted on wearing three-inch boots all the time, including today.

Astrid smirked and raised her camera. Snap. "Juxtaposition."

"Warn a hoe before you sneak up on me," he hissed. Astrid immediately burst into laughter.

Benny asked, "What's so funny?"

"You're my juxtaposition."

"What position, you dirty girl?"

"JUX-TA-PO-SI-TION. It means something ironic."

"So why'd you take a picture of me?"

"Benny, look at yourself. You're gayer than a French poodle wearing a pink beret. You're walking next to this stupid sugarcane field like you're on some twisted runway, and you have the nerve to question me, the irony. Army boots? Really?"

"Well, we are on a mission," he stated.

She shook her head in response, "What? To be the victim of a hate crime?"

"You know very well that none of those heathens will touch a hair on this glorious head. But onto more important things: Is he here? Did you talk to him yet?"

"Shut your hole, you damned blabbermouth."

He clasped his hands across his mouth dramatically. "You can't turn this off," he shuddered animatedly.

She chuckled. He could always make her smile. "No. I haven't seen him. I just got here myself."

"And you haven't been looking through your window to check if he was here?"

"I'm not a stalker, Benny."

"I sure as heck would be if I were hunting a fine fox. I'd be hiding behind a tapestry like Polonius in Hamlet. Heck, I'd wear the curtains."

"I'm not hunting," she snapped. "I guess you can call it window shopping."

"Window shopping. I like that. Makes you seem less slut-a-licious."

She slaps his shoulder. "I am not—that word."

"Well, lucky for you, I am. And I've got eagle eyes. Look over there, *something wicked this way comes*." He points to the cluster of fire engines.

Dylan Arias walked towards one of the fire engines wearing a brown, volunteer uniform. His shoulder-length, brown hair turned golden in the setting sun. He was taller than the others, standing over six-foot-one with sun-glazed skin. His bright smile was infectious. He was the life of the party, shaking hands and giving bro hugs to the other volunteers from the high school.When Dylan took out his cellphone, the other boys cheered. Astrid couldn't help but wonder what they were saying. Was it because some other girl had texted him? Someone more beautiful, more outgoing? Someone who shined? She felt a pang of jealousy, but quickly pushed it away. She took a deep breath and looked at her own nails, feeling a bit inadequate in comparison. Astrid lowered her camera.

Benny popped a piece of gum into his mouth and animatedly chewed his gum before blowing a bubble. "Jesus, you're right. I was wrong. He's hella-hot," he said in disbelief, fanning himself.

"I know," she agreed. "I could look at him all day."

"Have you even talked to him?"

"Yes. We talk," she explained. "Miss Bunny is always pairing us up, but Dylan doesn't think of me like that."

"Why?" he said.

"Our conversations are very superficial. Most guys don't have meaningful conversations, Benny."

"I do," he said.

"You're not like a guy-guy."

Benny pressed his lips together thinly. "Sorry if I don't conform to your backward gender stereotypes."

"Oh, please," scoffed Astrid. "Don't get all triggered on me. I'm just teasing you. And you know what I mean. Talking to you is easy. I'm not trying to smash you."

"Oh, Honeycakes, you'd be lucky to get your hands on all this deliciousness."

There was an awkward silence as Astrid gave Benny a deadpan glare. "Anywho, I'm going inside the field for a closer look and to get some shots."

"What!" he pointed to the sugarcane. "Like inside-INSIDE the field?"

"Yeah. Like maybe I can take a shot between the sugar cane stalks. You know, the sides can come out blurry with the focus on the fire trucks. I can spy and finish my homework at the same time."

"Are you crazy! They're going to light this bitch up in a few minutes. Did you see the tractor they are going to use? It's got flamethrowers, dude. It's like a John Deere dragon. Two minutes is all it takes to light this place up."

"Don't get your panties in a knot. The fire trucks aren't even on yet. I want a few shots. It will take two minutes."

"Astrid, don't be stupid. I'm not going after your ass if they start burning.

You can play the Latina Joan of Arc on your own time."

"Stop being dramatic. Save it for the plan."

"The plan!?" His eyebrows perked up.

"Yes. I've been planning it for a few days now."

"Girl, you can't just spring this on me. I need time to process things. I'm still not over my mom going blonde again."

"I don't tell you things because you're a blabbermouth, Benny."

"I'm not a blabber, I'm a blogger."

"You're a snitch is what you are, and you know it."

"My fans have a right to know about my life."

"You have eight followers—one of them is me."

"So what difference does it make who I tell? Hater. Hater. Spreading your damned Hater-aid."

"Listen, Benny. Run to Dylan and tell him you saw someone—probably me—wandering in the fields. When you come looking, I'll pretend to have fainted. He'll jump at the chance to play the hero. Trust me."

"You've got some messed up female logic there, Astrid."

"Oh, please. I've seen you stalk plenty of guys online trying to figure out what they like to get information on them. Remember when you pretended to like playing paintball because Sergio-what's-his-face did?"

"Oh yeah, never did get those neon stains out of my pink Burberry shirt."

She raised her eyebrows.

"You have a point, girl," he said. "But what if he doesn't want to come, or gets others to come, too. It might escalate."

She leaned in, "Look, he posts pictures of Superman all the time. He's just waiting for a chance to save the day."

"Astrid, I knew you had a storm brewing in your big old head, but this is like Hurricane force. Tsunami. You're like a Spanish Tornado. A tor-nah-do," he said in his best Antonio Banderas accent. "Girls are so conniving. I'd hate to see what happens to someone when they come after you."

"Dude, that's crazy. My mother literally told me the same thing half an hour ago."

"Well," he drawled. "She's psychic, isn't she?"

Astrid heard the sound of a loud muffler and turned to see a beast of a tractor inch its way towards the side of the field. Dylan and his group walked towards it. The burning of the sugarcane was about to begin.

Game on.

A Cord was Cut

ASTRID SLID INSIDE the sugarcane field. She was surprised Benny hadn't commented on her perfume. If her best friend didn't notice it, why would Dylan? This is pure desperation, isn't it? *I'm so freaking pathetic,* she thought as the sun's rays began lowering in the distance.

I think I'm the only person on this whole stupid earth to develop this idea. Is this a good idea? Probably not, but I was sure this would be the only thing to get Dylan's attention. That's why when he accepted my Friend Request (I know, total desperate move), I scrolled all the way down his entire page looking for information on him. Thank goodness boys are about as giving as old dairy cows. There wasn't much to scroll through, but I did find a nice little cartoon about fifteen posts in. It was Superman, and he was flying and carrying some girl to safety. Typical. What is it about superheroes? Does Dylan think he's inferior or weak in some way? What can I do to make him feel special? Be his kryptonite. No! Wait. That would kill him! Whatever power it is that makes Superman SUPER. That's what I've got to be.

Would Dylan even come? Would any of this even matter? I hope that nut bag Benny will be able to deliver. I hope he doesn't see his reflection before he finds Dylan. Time is of the essence. I can't believe how long he stares at himself on any reflective surface. God, I'm so relieved I didn't tell him. He's such a friggin' blabbermouth. She blew a few strands of hair from her eyes and raised her camera. *Guess we'll find out. Where the heck am I? How far have I gone?*

Each step she took deeper into the field brought new sounds. *Maybe I should stop.* The dead foliage cracked underneath, and small plants snapped as she stepped over them. It was colder in the field, an arid scent penetrated the area. It smelled like angry rain. She hadn't walked more than ten paces but felt as though she were deep within the field already. *I didn't turn. I've been going straight. I was coming in from the South, and I'm facing North. North?* Astrid hadn't realized the sugar cane was so tall, much taller than she was. Just over six feet, most things were taller than she was. But as she ventured through the dense stalks, she wondered if the canes were growing taller and taller, inching their way over her, making the fading sun die faster and faster.

She removed her phone from her jacket. Dead. No signal. *The hell?* A strange cold breeze rattled the sugar cane plants, causing a loud rustling of leaves. It sounded like a million cicadas were singing at once. *Animals! There are animals in the field.* The thought hadn't occurred to her before. A queasy coldness grew in her stomach. A therapist once told her to tap the sides of her wrist whenever she felt fear or anxiety. Immediately, her fingers began tap-tap-tapping away at the sides of her hand, but this did not calm her fears. What was she thinking? Maybe she should have planned this through a bit more. There had to be animals in the field, rodents and bugs, and every creature in between. Bugs weren't the issue. She wasn't a girly girl, but the rats were something that might make her scream. And then there were the snakes. She heard what sounded like a rattle close to her feet and immediately felt her heart start to pound. *What was that!? No-no-no-no.* She was terrified of snakes, especially the ones that didn't warn before the strike. Her eyes shot down towards her feet. But everything was suddenly so dark. Feeling like a broken camera, she was focusing and trying to discern what was happening in front of her. Anything. The blur was maddening. She needed to know what that noise was! Astrid spun around and felt the sugar cane cut her forearm. "Shit," she cringed, wiping away a bit of blood. *I'm only a few feet in! Abort mission!*

She bolted in the direction she came from but was struck by a heaviness in her chest. *Where is it? Where's the edge? It was only a few feet. It was only like six feet. Wasn't it?*

Astrid had come into the field from the Southernmost part. So she had to turn North. That's where she came from. It was the South, wasn't it? The sun sets in the west. But the stars were off that night. *How did it get so dark so fast?* Blackness filled the sky. She looked at her phone and could barely see its white cover. She could scarcely see anything at all. *Benny!* There was blackness all around her. She looked up, but the plants were tall. These shadowy figures looked like angry hands reaching for the black sky. And they were growing!

Her camera felt heavier and heavier. Using her camera's flash, she guided herself through the dark field using the light from the SLR. She rammed through some stalks, hoping to find the fire engines. Any signs of light. Any flicker of life outside the area. Nothing but rows of sugarcane stared back at her. The field swayed sinisterly in the light breeze. She turned the other way, spreading apart more stalks. This time she sprinted. More of her flesh was cut as she cried in pain. No end in sight! The realization thundered in her chest. She went in too far and was utterly lost. What had she gotten herself into?

The Latina Joan of Arc, that's what they'll call me when they find me.

A horn in the distance gave her some hope, and she lunged towards the sound, breaking stalks and scratching at her face as she forced herself through a self-made path. Astrid burrowed through the sugar cane. *This was a mistake*, she thought. *This was a terrible mistake!* Then the sirens blasted. The noise made her freeze. It wasn't a warning-it was a promise. The promise of fire. She'd heard it every time she watched the men burn the sugarcane fields. Astrid suddenly found her mind spinning, the thoughts blasting loudly within. *The sirens mean fire.* And she was in the field.

Run!

The clatter of men intensified as the beeping and sirens echoed. Her throat was dry now. It was a horror she hadn't experienced before, imminent and real. Astrid's breathing intensified as she ran through the stalks for what seemed an eternity.

"Benny," she cried. "BENNY!" Screaming was so painful! *My God*, her throat had never been so dry and her heart had never felt the thud of such fear.

A flash of light came from her North. The fire was coming! Terror grew in her eyes. The bright red light grew taller and wider almost instantly as it barrelled its way through the stalks. The horrible cracking sound with an intense crescendo. The light was coming. But the light came from the fire, and it was coming straight towards her. The burning had begun.

The fire came from the North. Yes, that's where they were. All of them, the fire trucks and the men and Benny. He had to have reached Dylan by now, and they were looking for her. But where was she? A heavy plume of smoke cascaded towards her, foul and powerful. "BENNY HELP!" Her voice croaked. It was hard to breathe and even harder to see. Running away from the smoke was her only option. My God, this was a never-ending maze! The stalks were growing instantly around her, taunting her, cutting her with their razor-sharp leaves.

A rabid ferocity took over her chest as it rose and fell. She tripped on a stalk in the dizzying whirl, causing her body to crash to the ground. Struggling to rise, she caught a glimpse of something in the smoke around her. In the blackness of the haze was a pair of glowing eyes staring at her from the ground. Her blood turned to ice. Then she heard the horrible rattling sound, a menacing noise that echoed in her mind.

Her limbs were tingling, but her eyes were like coals. Every muscle in her body refused to move. It was as if every star in the heavens had crashed inside her and were pulsating wildly. Astrid felt the familiar stars and static, the black and white sprinkles of a broken television. Every cell of her body was made of fire and ice. The heaviness of her body pounded the ground. She didn't know how, but this had happened before, and she thought as if this terrible moment would never pass. The breaths came in and out in manic jerks. Screaming was impossible. All she could do was focus on the glowing eyes.

Trapped in her body and vividly conscious, she knew there was something in the sugarcane field staring at her. "Help me, please." The mind or the spirit cried out. A few tears escaped her eyes, cleaning away the dirt on her face. An even stranger sensation overtook her. The static and stars abruptly stopped. Then she felt herself rise and the weight of nothingness lifted her. It was like she was having another lucid dream. But this time, she wasn't sleeping—it was real. Suddenly, the pain stopped. Something snapped. A cord was cut, taking her out of her body. After a while, she felt her spirit float her higher and higher until she was looking beyond the sugar cane field.

Colors were different in this state. From the blackness and fog of darkness came brilliant surreal purple and blue hues. A new reality took hold of her. Astrid looked down at the thing with the glowing eyes as the form followed her ascension. Between the stalks, between the sugarcane and the approaching fire was a dark presence. A sinister, serpentine form. The burning eyes were angry. Through her new perspective, she could vividly identify the long snake. Her altered state gave the animal an eerie yellow glow. It must have easily been at least six feet in length. The snake raised its thick body upward and hissed maniacally. It's rattler shook violently.

Astrid scanned past the snake, at the dozen men around the perimeter of the field. The image she saw was crisp and hyper-defined. Every particle was crystal clear, even the strange orbs of light surrounding the men as they patrolled the grounds. Their bodies were a sea of neon colors.

Then she saw towards the three fire trucks, and spotted Benny still running toward her body below. The embers were rising and floating past her, carried by the wind. Below, she saw her pale body sprawled on the floor. Immobile and vulnerable. The strange snake was no more than five feet away from her. The emptiness of her eyes reflected the cold night sky. Suddenly, the snake lowered its head and began slithering closer to her body.

Astrid. A deep, sweet voice echoed all around her.

The snake inched closer

Astrid, Mi hija. Familiar and kind.

Grandma! She felt the words resonate inside her. But this wasn't inside. She was OUTSIDE! How do thoughts exist outside of the body? How does anything live outside of form? She was weightless, tingly, a new form of energy.

Don't be afraid, said the familiar voice in Spanish, her grandmother Carmen's voice. The words thundered everywhere, rattling her soul. *I am with you.*

She felt the snake's tongue flick against her arm.

Astrid's spirit trembled. Somewhere deep inside her, she knew that snake wasn't natural. Neither of them was a part of this world. Her heart pounded with fear.

Be strong. Haste fuerte, the voice thundered. *You are not bound to your skin.* *YOU ARE NOT BOUND TO YOUR SKIN!*

The blue snake raised its head and rattled its tail again. When it was about to strike at her arm, a bolt of light fell out of the sky. A white thunderbolt struck Astrid, enveloping her whole: body, mind and spirit. Light rushed through her veins in less than a second, filling her arteries with radiant energy and white charge. The animal wriggled, flipping its body until it disappeared from sight. Then all at once, the light turned black. Nothing was nothing again.

Astrid was back in her shell.

Petrichor

"WHAT WERE YOU THINKING?!" a voice hollered as tiny lights flickered in her eyes. Astrid's lungs felt like anvils. She felt tingly all over, as if she had slept on every limb. As if she were living static. But how was that possible? *Not again*, the dark thought came quickly. *Not again.* The sound was a cacophony of sirens in the distance, static and muffled voices. *Has this happened before? Why did it feel so familiar?* Why was the thought so painful?

"Are you alright?" She knew the voice. She knew it well.

Benny. It's Benny. Why was she so prickly all over!

Astrid felt a heaviness in her head, a thick black fog of confusion.

"Girl." She heard the words clearly now. "No, don't get help, you idiot. No need to cause drama. Can't you see she's only fallen," said her best friend. *Benny is my best friend. Benny and I have known each other since we were little children. Why is my mouth so dry?* Astrid could feel someone's hands on hers. She could feel a pulse. Her veins felt the pumping. It was movement—power rushing within her.

The voice was louder now, still foggy, but louder. "I'm the dramatic one, not you. Quit freaking out on me. Give Astrid a God-damned moment, Dylan." The voice was even clearer now: "Girl, get up!" Benny screeched. "Hello. Wake up, Diva."

Astrid felt her arms now. They were strong, and Astrid used this strength to push her torso up. The images were beginning to clear. Her throat, dry and cracking on the inside, was about to produce sound. She knew the words were coming; she had to give her body time. "Wh-"

"Jesus, can't you see she needs some god-damned water, Dylan. Move your ass!" Benny snapped.

Astrid took a deep breath. It felt as if this had been the first breath she had ever taken. The oxygen rushed to reach every cell of her. "What happened?" she mustered the weak question.

"We found you on the ground. You dumb-dumb! What the hell is wrong with you?"

A tall figure crouched next to her with a bottle of water.

"Drink it, bitch," ordered Benny.

She opened her mouth and felt the figure cup her chin tenderly, as if her chin were the head of a newborn baby.

"Yes, drink, please," said a deeper voice. A familiar sound. *Dylan's voice!* The water tasted like liquid gold. She needed this. She was alive, and her throat was working. The cold water slid down into her stomach where it woke her core. Her lips were wet now and she ran her tongue around them. She was part of this world again.

"What happened?" she repeated, much stronger this time.

"We found you on the damn ground!" Benny shook his head. "You're lucky we found you when we did. They started burning the field, you dumb hoe!"

"Burning," she whispered. Dylan was staring down at her. His eyes avoided hers as he crossed his arms over his chest.

She immediately tried to stand up. Benny helped her.

"Are you, are you alright?" asked Dylan. Still no eye contact.

"Yes," she nodded frantically. "Yes. I'm fine. Thank you."

Benny crossed his arms, then puckered his face to the side and gave her his best, "I can't believe you put me through this" face.

"You know you shouldn't have done that," mumbled Dylan. "Gone into the field like that." He rubbed the back of his neck. Their eyes met, "You could have gotten hurt."

"Yes," she said faintly. "Yes, I know."

"Why did you do it?" asked Dylan.

"I-I-don't know."

"She wanted a picture," blurted Benny.

"A picture?" replied Dylan.

Benny raised his eyebrow. "A damned picture, and not even for Instagram. For the stupid yearbook. For that fat Miss Bunny!"

"For school," she protested. Her throat was hoarse. So dry!

Dylan gave a half-smirk. "Well, you better get an 'A' for that one. I'll tell Ms. Bunny how dedicated you are."

She chuckled nervously.

"I'm glad that you're alright, Astrid," he placed both hands in his pocket. "I—uh, I've gotta go. You sure you don't need me to send someone? We probably should get you checked just in case."

"No. No. I'll be fine. It must have been the smoke. I'll be fine."

"She'll be alright, Dylan," interjected Benny. "You go on and play with your hose now. Thanks for being a good boy with the water. Run along, run along now."

"Umm. Alright. See you around. Glad you're OK."

Seeing Dylan out of earshot, Benny snapped his head. "Girl, you're so full of it!"

"What do you mean?"

"Oh… it must have been the smoke." He cackled. "We should give you an award for the way you threw yourself on the floor. I don't know how you held your breath for so long—best dead girl impression ever. Your stomach and chest didn't go up or anything. I bet you were screaming inside when Dylan gave you mouth to mouth! Dirty girl!"

Mouth? Dylan? Me? "What are you talking about!?"

"And you were so convincing. I need to take drama lessons from *you*. The way you laid there motionless when that hunk of junk was all up in your business giving you the breath of all sorts of life."

She pressed her fingers to her lips. "Mouth to mouth?" She scanned the floor. "Benny, I don't remember that happening."

Benny scoffed. "The cameras are off, Girl. No need to keep up the charade."

"Benny, I'm serious. The last thing I remember was floating. I don't know. Like I wasn't me anymore. It was like a dream I had the other night. Like I couldn't feel anymore. I knew I was afraid, but I couldn't control my body.

Didn't you see the bolt of lightning! The lights! I heard my grandmother's voice. I mean ACTUALLY heard it… it wasn't a dream," her voice drifted as an image flashed in her mind's eye. You are not bound to your skin.

The snake. The fire. Then came the whiteness.

"I saw a snake in there!" she confessed.

"Jesus!"

"It crawled next to me, Benny." I didn't feel it, but I saw it. I saw its tongue."

"That's insane!"

"Something happened in the field, Benny. Something. I think something found me."

ASTRID WAS QUIET FOR MOST of the walk home. She didn't know how to explain what happened in the field or the terrible thing she saw or the fear that plagued her. How could she expect Benny to believe her? She wasn't sure if she believed it herself. I *would have known if Dylan Arias had been kissing me. I mean, I've wanted to taste his lips for three years. I would know if they were on mine. I can't believe I don't remember any of it. It would be just my luck: to have the boy of my dreams save my life and not even be conscious enough to realize it. But was it real? Was it a dream? I don't know! It makes no sense to me.* She looked at Benny, who appeared deep in thought as well. *He probably thinks I've gone crazy*, she thought to herself. *Maybe I have.*

A few drops of rain started to fall over them. Benny turned to her and smiled.

"I love the smell of rain," Astrid said, breaking the silence.

"It's called Petrichor," he replied.

"Is it?"

"Yes. I'm not just a pretty face, you know," he grinned. "I googled it once, and I liked the word: Petrichor."

"Petrichor," she repeated, smiling back.

"It's Greek. Means the mixture of stone and the blood of the gods."

"Wow. That's a beautiful definition."

"It is. It reminds me of you."

She stopped. "What do you mean?"

"Well, you're like a stone: you're hard and you're constant." He smiled. "And there is something extra special about you. I've always known this. I think you have God's blood in you."

Despite her best efforts, Astrid's eyes started to water. "Benny, I don't know what to say. That's the nicest thing anyone's ever said to me."

He nodded. "And I like the way you smell," he continued to walk. "Don't think I didn't notice the perfume you're wearing."

"You're the sweetest person I've ever met, too."

"Shame we're not compatible," he said. "We'd be the power couple to end all power couples. I hope Dylan Arias sees how great you are."

As tears fell from her eyes, she reached for his arm. "Benny, I really do think I saw something in the field. Something weird happened to me. I don't think it was a panic attack. I don't think I blacked out. I think I—," she shook her head, "I actually think I woke up." She widened her eyes, "Please believe me."

He gave a sympathetic smile then placed his hands on her shoulders. "My mother told me a story about you a while back. That's the reason she stopped letting me come over about four years ago. Apparently, we were playing. I guess you had come over or something; you know how we've always been together. She said it was some time after your granny died. My mother used to have your granny read her cards; she's the only person she ever truly trusted to do those things with. And while we were playing, you wandered off into the brush, and we were looking for you for a while. Apparently, it was a long while. I don't remember any of this, mind you, but mom told me the story again one night when she had a little too much Jesus Juice. She asked me why I liked you so much when all of you were a bunch of witches. Bad people. Devil people."

"But not bad enough to avoid. I remember your mother was always visiting my granny."

"True Felton's. We take whatever is convenient and discard whatever we feel is bad. Anyway, she said we found you in a clearing behind our house."

"I don't remember anything from my childhood, to be honest."

"You don't want to remember this, girl. She said there was a ring of snakes circling you." He drew a circle with his finger.

"Jesus Christ."

"That's what she said. Of course she ran away. She said she felt horrible for leaving you, but she was terrified. That's why she says that my gayness was probably residue from your granny's magic, that your illness was also a residue. That's what attracted the snakes. She said it was a punishment. But I knew better."

"What," she looked deep into his blue eyes. "What did you know?"

"You have it, too. Maybe not like your granny. But you've got magic, too."

Astrid exhaled deeply.

"And maybe," he continued. "Maybe it did find you tonight." He reached for her hand and forced a reassuring smile. "But you want to know what I think? I think whatever it was you saw tonight should be afraid of you."

"Why? I don't understand why anything would be scared of me."

"Because you've got God's blood in you."

"Benny, we all have God's blood. God made us in his image."

"Yeah," he said. "But God has made you special. He made you stand out. I wish you embraced who you are. You weren't meant to be behind a camera. You were meant to shine. Let your light shine, girl. As Hamlet said to Ophelia, 'God has given you one face, and you make yourself another.'" He shook his finger. "Don't deny who you are. Don't deny what's inside you. Don't deny your magic."

Astrid sighed deeply. "I love it when you quote Shakespeare. Please don't judge me, Benny. We've both had to hide parts of who we are," she wiped tears from her eyes.

"Facts, hoe," he reached for her hand and squeezed it tight. "Pure facts."

59

The Hazards of Witch Blood

A STRID PEEKED INSIDE her house through the porch window. Sarah was sitting in the living room using her cell phone with her back facing the front door. "Crap. Mom's still awake. I didn't want to see her."

"Why?" Benny shoved his face close to the screen. Astrid impatiently pushed him back.

"She's going to know you fool."

"Know?"

"She *always* knows, Benny. Before I open my mouth, she always finds out when something is wrong. I'm surprised she didn't end up running to the field with a machete after that snake. It's like a Batman sign lights up the sky whenever something bad happens to me."

"The hazards of witch blood." He said in a slow, zombie voice.

"You're not funny," she scoffed. "I thought you said it was God's blood."

"Same thing," he quipped.

"I don't want to deal with this right now," she grunted. "Let's hope she doesn't ask too many questions," she turned and pointed at Benny. "Don't open your big fat mouth. I don't want her to find out what happened."

Benny pinched his mouth and zipped his lips shut with a flowy stroke. "Like a grave," he said.

She reluctantly opened the door and called from the entrance with an "I'm home," then let the screen door slam behind her and Benny.

"How was it?" Sarah didn't lift her head.

"Good-good," she insisted. "It was good. I got lots of pictures. Gonna go upload them. For the project," she muttered.

"Alright, baby. Night," said Sarah. That was easy. Benny made a "Hello, introduce me. What am I a freaking ghost?" face. She rolled her eyes, "Benny came for a visit." Astrid said.

"Benny!" Sarah jolted her head up and tossed her cell phone on the table. "My other baby!" she exclaimed

Astrid's eyes turned into slits. She mouthed the words "Not one word," at Benny before going up the stairs.

Benny flashed a great grin towards Sarah. "Hey pretty girl," he said and walked into the kitchen.

"I was wondering when I'd see you again," Sarah cupped his face in her hands and gave him a kiss on the cheek. "Ever since school started, you never come around anymore."

Astrid clasped her hands together. "I'm gonna be upstairs. You guys catch up."

"Night, hon," replied Sarah, not lifting her gaze off Benny.

Astrid mouthed the words, "NOT ONE WORD," at Benny before going out of sight.

He leaned against the small kitchen table. "I've had rehearsals, Sarah."

"Oh yeah… what's this year's play?" Sara asked while pulling up a chair.

"Yeah. It's 'Grease'. I'm playing Rizzo."

"Rizzo," her eyes lit up and her smile widened.

"Just kidding. I'm working with costumes and makeup, and occasionally I'm an 'Extra'."

She reached for his hand. "My Benny is not 'Extra' material."

"Right! The only thing I'm extra at is being Extra Special."

Sarah nodded. "Never forget that. How's your dad treating you since you told him—"

"—That his Benny likes boys?" He pulled up a chair next to her.

She brushed a strand of blue hair from his forehead and gave him a gentle pat on his knee. Sarah abruptly reached for his hand, flipping it over to reveal his left-hand wrist. Sarah inspected it. "Now the other one."

He grunted, reluctantly showing his right side as well.

"You can't even see them anymore." She touched his forearm tenderly.

Benny pulled back his arms, "I don't do that anymore. I stopped. That's not something you need to worry about. The doctor said I'm better."

Sarah touched his shoulder. "I'm glad to hear that. I was worried about you for a while there. We all were. Astrid especially. I'm sure you know that. It was just a bad time. We all have rough patches."

He nodded and half-smiled. "It was one time. I think my mom caused a scene for nothing. They were just little scratches. A couple of cuts because I was bored. My mom and dad blew it out of proportion." He scoffed, "Lesson learned—always lock your doors while Regina Felton is home."

"That's not funny. Hurting yourself is not something you want to joke about. You be careful and come talk to me if you're ever—how did you call it—bored."

"Kids are so dramatic," he said.

"Dramatic and stupid. Unaware of the consequences of their actions."

He sighed loudly. "I get it. I messed up, Sarah. Can we move on, please?"

She nodded. "You're right," she forced a smile. "How's your dad?"

"He doesn't talk to me much," shrugged Benny. "He stays away. I don't mind it. Lately all we do is text, but it's kind of a good thing. He won't even look at me, didn't even tell me anything about my hair when I colored it. He saw it, kind of scoffed and walked out the door. He texted me an hour later saying he thinks I should reconsider my hair' choices.' I don't know. He likes me from a distance, I guess. My dad likes the idea of me—the idea of having me around, having me on his contacts, and getting my texts. But the idea of having to listen to my voice and look at my face sets him off somehow. He doesn't mind the idea of me, but he certainly doesn't care for what I represent. I really don't like it when he drinks. That's the only time he really talks to me. But talking leads to screaming."

Sarah reached for his hands, assuring him. "What about your Mom? I've known her a long time, and she seems like a very open woman. Very loving. What does she do when he tells you things?"

"Loving?" he scoffed. "Where did this cliche of an overbearing mother creating a gay child come from? She's been nothing but distant. She's nice to you because she's a Felton, and we have a certain name to uphold, but she's frigid and distant. My dad used to be more loving than her. Crazy wants me to find a girlfriend. Can you believe that? Regina Felton, in all her uppity glory, came into my bedroom about four nights ago and demanded I find a girlfriend." Benny raised his hands in the air. "She literally found me making out with a guy in my bedroom not more than two months ago and has the audacity to tell me to find a girl. I mean, what kind of lunatic would demand something like that? Who cares what people think? I'm here and queer, and this is the twenty-first century. What's the damned problem?"

"Well, the Felton's have a name to uphold around here. Judges. Lawyers. They don't want these small minds to judge you."

"Some name," he scoffed. "Half my family is in jail, and the others aren't locked up because they were too smart to get caught. Or they bribed the right judge. Or they *were* the right judge. A bunch of crooks and thieves."

"Don't talk bad about your family, Benjamin Lee Felton. Whatever they are… they're part of your blood."

"Well then, apparently I've got some incurable and nasty ass leukemia. I think my blood is poisoned AF."

Sarah shook her head and sighed. "You're so melodramatic. You're exactly like Astrid. I can see why you two are good friends."

"Everyone needs drama. It fuels the soul."

"Then you two have enough fuel to skyrocket right out of here," joked Sarah. "You know, my momma used to tell me stories about people like you."

"Like me?" said Benny.

"Yeah. About boys who like boys and girls who like girls."

"Can't help who you like. Too bad I don't like Astrid. Her feet are too big, and she farts in her sleep."

"Benny, you're so silly. I know you didn't choose this life. My momma told me people like you were extra special."

"Why?" he asked.

"Because you are double-spirited."

"What does that mean?"

"It means you have the power to carry both the masculine and the feminine spirit inside you. You are not bound to one gender. You can be both. You can live two lives if you want. You can exist twice."

"Interesting."

"Momma never lied. You are extra special. Never forget that."

Benny's eyes beamed, "Why can't all moms be like you?"

Sarah brushed her thick hair to the side. "I'd be grateful if you could share that with Astrid for me. She didn't dignify herself to come to kiss me goodnight. She ran upstairs. Little turd doesn't know I'd burn the world for her if I had to. It's different for moms and their girls. You always feel like you have to say the right thing or everything is going to fall apart. A girl's life can change in a heartbeat. One wrong move and it creates a spiral. But I pray for her. I'm not like other mothers who make a show about those things. I'm not as affectionate as my mom was with Astrid. I had her so young. I didn't know what I was doing. To be perfectly honest, I still don't. I pray for her, though. I do. Every night I pray for my little Astrid," she laughed. "Just like I'm sure your mom prays for her little turd, too."

"No. Astrid loves you. She loves you very much."

"I know, I'm teasing you. Did everything turn out alright at the burning?"

"Oh yeah. I'm sure Astrid will be fine."

"Fine?" said Sarah, looking surprised by his response. "What do you mean she'll be fine? Who? Who will be fine?"

"Oh, she had a little slip—" Benny stuttered.

"—Slip?" Sarah became rattled and her eyes widened. "Astrid? Well, why didn't she tell me? Are you sure she's OK?"

"Yeah, she fell a little, is all," he backpedaled, nodding intensely. "Dummy was looking through her camera when she walked smack into a hole in the ground. Twisted her foot, I think."

"Benny, you're not telling me something."

"No, she's fine," he squealed. "Really."

Sarah scanned Benny with her eyes.

He grimaced. "Fine," he finally exhaled. "Astrid was trying to get some guys attention.

"Dylan Aria?"

"Yeah. That guy. She thought she could make a hero out of him (her words not mine), so she went into the field when they set it on fire."

"She what!"

"Not too far in. Astrid wanted Dylan to feel like Superman."

Sarah's mouth dropped a bit. "What the hell goes on in your minds? She could have burned!"

"But we found her. She was convincing, too. She pretended to stop breathing. I honestly don't know how she did it. She looked dead. Like dead-dead. Astrid must have gotten into character because she said she felt like she was floating."

"Floating?" Sarah's eyes widened.

"Yeah."

"She said that?" A cold fear flushed Sarah's face.

"Yeah. Weird."

Sarah didn't say a word.

"Listen, I should probably get going. My mother's going to start calling if I don't come home soon."

"Oh, sure. Sure. Thank you for watching my baby."

"Yeah, she was scared and didn't want to bother you with this. I think some tea will calm her down."

"I'm sure it will. I'll take her some and talk to her in a minute."

"Don't tell her I told you anything. Please. I promised her I wouldn't. You know how she is. I'll never hear the end of it."

She forced a smile. "I won't, *mijo*."

Benny hugged her, then quickly left home.

As soon as Benny was out of sight, Sarah reached for her phone. Her voice trembled. "It's me. I think it happened. I think Astrid knows. No. NO. Listen to me. Stop. Stop. Listen for once! Come home. Something happened. I sensed it coming—I told you I sensed it. I told you something was coming and you blew me off like you always blow me off. No. No. I don't care. Come back. You've gotta come back. Momma's not here to protect us. I'm not strong enough and they don't play fair. You know I've never been strong. No! Astrid can't! How can you suggest that! She can't and she shouldn't. It's you. It has to be you." Sarah was in tears, red and flustered. "Please come home… Marianne. I need you. WE need you."

The Filth in Our Darlings

I N A STRANGE WAY, Sarah understood why Benny's father avoided him. Despite her unwillingness to disown a child for something as innocuous as sexuality, she understood the concept well. She was perfectly comfortable looking at her daughter and listening to her voice, but all the dark parts didn't need to be known to her. Sarah was perfectly content in listening to Astrid's sarcastic jokes and sharing personal stories but she didn't necessarily need to hear all the sordid details. Was this wrong of her? She thought of the phrase "ignorance is bliss." But this wasn't ignorance, this was downright stupidity. How could she not know the thing she carried? How could she not feel it? *I don't need to know all the bad stuff you carry,* thought Sarah. *The world is so ugly. We don't need to see the filth in our darlings.* At that moment, she knew something terrible needed to be buried.

She gently drummed on the door of Astrid's bedroom before slowly opening it. The computer cast an eerie blue hue in the familiar bright yellow room while Astrid worked at her desk. While she uploaded the pictures from her camera to her laptop, Astrid noticed how they were all somewhat distorted. The one "Juxtaposition" shot she took of Benny had a green glow around him. She tried hard not to think about the night's events. "You still awake, baby?" Sarah whispered from behind.

"Yeah." she rubbed her eyes. "Trying to figure out why these photos look so bad. I think the sensor is broken. Where's Benny?"

"He went home. Let's get that camera taken care of in the morning," Sarah stepped closer.

"All the pictures come out fuzzy. All these weird colors keep popping up, even when it's completely dark."

"Well, you're the expert on that. I wouldn't know anything about it."

"I'm no expert. It's just a hobby. I still use Automatic Mode most of the time, mom."

"Still, it's something you're passionate about. I'm thrilled you have a passion. Having hobbies is good for you."

Astrid scrunched her forehead. "Are you feeling alright?" she asked.

Sarah forced a smile then stepped closer to her daughter. She removed Astrid's glasses and turned her face towards hers, noting the small cuts on her face and arm. "Astrid, I know we don't always share everything that goes on in our lives, but I don't like secrets. I need you to be honest with me about something."

"I'm getting nervous. What's going on?"

"Nothing," she smiled weakly. "I want you to tell me if anything weird happened tonight. I want to know if something strange happened at the Felton Fields."

"Nope. Nothing out of the ordinary."

Sarah bit her lip and nodded intently. "Oh. I'm wondering because your pants are all dirty and you came straight up here—why do you have all these cuts on your face?"

"Oh, that…I tripped. I scraped my knee a bit."

Sarah's smile went away. "Astrid, your knees are fine, and you know it."

Astrid leaned back on her chair and crossed her arms. "How did you find out? The blabbermouth cards or the blabbermouth Benny?"

"Don't get smart with me, Astrid. He was concerned about you. And he should be."

"The Blabbermouth Benny," she said under her breath.

"It's a good thing he told me. I'm glad he blabbed. What possessed you to go into the field? What the hell is wrong with you?"

"I was just taking pictures." She scrolled through her photos. "See? Schoolwork."

"He told me you fell. Did something else happen? Don't lie to me."

Astrid raised her voice, "Mom, nothing happened."

"Benny said you told him you were floating. Floating."

"Benny's a moron who thinks he looks good with blue hair. Why would you give what he says an ounce of thought?"

"Well, that may very well be, but how would he know to say that unless it came out of your mouth?"

"Oh my God! Benny is a walking novel! He always makes up stories."

"Benny is dramatic, but he's not a liar. Astrid, be serious. What happened out there? Tell me. I don't like secrets."

"That's all we have." Astrid muttered under her breath.

"What was that?" Sarah snapped back.

"Nothing!"

"Tell me what happened. Open your damned mouth."

"I don't know," she flailed her arms in the air then moved to her bed. "I can't make sense of it. How can I tell you something I'm not even sure happened?"

"Honey, if something happened in the field, I need to know exactly what happened. You can't be playing around when strange things happen to you."

"It happened fast," she mumbled. "I went into the field to take pictures and then I felt uneasy. Scared. I thought I could see something looking at me. Something with red eyes and then I got all tingly. Like when your foot falls asleep. I thought I was having an anxiety attack, so I tried to calm down, but this was different. It felt like every part of my body was asleep, but I was awake. Very, awake. Then I saw myself lying on the floor of the field. I heard grandma's voice. I heard her just like I'm hearing you. She was in the field with me. What scared me most was when I saw the snake. A long one. It was so creepy looking. Blue. A weird blue color. It wasn't natural." She widened her eyes. "To be honest, I don't think it's the first time I've seen them. Can you dream of things before you actually see them?

Sarah's eyes were wet. "Astrid." Her hands were trembling.

"Mom," she said softly, "What happened out there? What was that thing? I know you can tell me," she leaned towards Sarah. "Maybe you could use your cards to tell me. Just this once," she pleaded.

Sarah turned away. "Astrid, I can't do that for you. I can't read your cards. I've tried before. We've been over this."

"Why not? You read other people's cards. Why not your own daughter? This is something I want to understand. It's getting me scared."

"Because what happened in those fields has nothing to do with your future, honey. It's not going to affect you in any way. Don't claim it. Forget it. Forget what you think you saw, Astrid. It's better this way."

"You want me to forget one of the—no, THE— weirdest thing to ever happen to me? Really? Snap. Just like that… Forget? Is there a little pill you'd like me to take again as well?" She scoffed. "I bet Grandma would have told me. You're a coward. Afraid to face reality. Afraid to face your sisters. Afraid to face life. Some fortune teller you turned out to be. Can't even see how sad and scared you truly are."

"Astrid," she tried remaining calm. "You don't have a gift. It's something you've always wanted. You would ask me why you couldn't read cards or be like your grandma even as a child. You forget these things, but I've seen you playing with my cards. I know you've done research on magic. But the gifts didn't pass. It's not for everyone. Don't you think it would have manifested by now? I'm sorry, Astrid, but you don't. Stop looking for something that isn't there."

"I'm sorry, but that's a terrible thing to say to someone. You don't have the gift. How can you say that?"

"Astrid, do you think I like having to deal with other people's problems? It seems exciting to be part of this world, but believe me, honey, you are blessed. Blessed to have a quiet mind and a quiet soul. Don't go looking for things that don't exist. You are blessed not to have this burden. I wish I didn't have this gift."

Astrid paused for a moment. "Grandma told me I was blessed. She told me I was blessed eternally. I remember her telling me." Astrid nodded. "She said I was special. I did hear her voice tonight."

"She meant you were lucky you didn't have any gifts. You know how she suffered. I don't have to tell you about what happened when other *brujas* retaliated after she healed people and removed their enchantments. You are blessed not to have to deal with this burden. That is special. Get that through your head."

"No, no, that's not what she meant. She said God has blessed me eternally. She said I could ride the wind."

"Ride the Wind. What does that even mean?" she said, containing her laughter.

"You're such a bitch," she said. "I can't believe you are laughing at me. I wish I were out of my body right now."

Sarah suddenly slapped Astrid across the face, causing Sarah to immediately flinch back. "Astrid, I'm sorry. I didn't mean to!"

The right side of her cheek burned. A rage gathered inside her. How could her mother be so cruel! So violent! "Get out!" She thundered.

Panic came over Sarah as she recoiled towards the door. "Astrid. I'm sorry. I didn't mean to!"

Tears welled in Astrid's eye. "Get out!" Astrid thundered and slammed the door as her mother stepped out. Astrid felt her body tingle with rage. She sat on her bed, her heart pounding, as the familiar prickly sensation of static worked its way throughout her body. This time, she didn't try to stop the strange feeling. Astrid let the rage flow.

Ride the Wind

HOW COULD ASTRID possibly sleep with everything that just happened? The fire. The eyes. The strange snake she saw in the field. Hearing her grandmother's voice. The soaring. Then the slap. The quintessential, Stereotypical Latino Slap! *I don't understand why my mom would get so crazy. So angry that she hit me. HIT me. I don't think she's ever done that before.* She sat up from her bed, walked to her window facing the Felton fields, and pulled apart the curtains. *What happened out there?* "What was that?" the words escaped. "What the hell is going on with me?"

Astrid replayed the events of the night over and over in her mind's eye. She thought about how she felt when she saw those terrible eyes in the sugarcane field and how scared they made her. But at this point, she couldn't be sure of anything. Maybe they were reflections. Everything was so muddy—so chaotic. Perhaps the snake was a hose? The sound of rattling was a rumble from the tractors. The light she thought came from above might have been a beam from a Border Patrol helicopter. But no, the light was much too bright to be a simple light—it was too powerful to be of this world. Maybe it came from the blimp, the one run by the Border Patrol with the infrared lights. They say it can see bodies at night of people trying to cross the river, even when there is no moon. *Was there a moon tonight?* She couldn't remember. What about her grandmother's voice? How did that fit into the equation? The thunderous voice! Why did she remember being up there, in the sky, and looking down? Why did she feel like she was floating? Didn't she? How was she able to see Benny and Dylan running to the rescue? Did she hallucinate the whole thing? And why couldn't Astrid remember his lips on hers? You would think she would remember something as vital as that. She tried to concentrate and pick her brain, looking for a fragment from the past. What would her grandmother have said if she had explained the night's events? Abuela Carmen would probably call on angels or the wind. "There are answers all around us," the old woman would probably say, "We have to listen with our hearts."

But how can she listen to anything with this thundering mind? How can answers come to a mind spinning with questions and...rage? Yes. There was rage, too. Lots of it! *Mom. Why would she hit me like that?*

I do want to leave my body. I wish I could just get out of my bones and away from her! Is that what it was? Maybe this is what Grandma was talking about. Maybe that's why mom was so angry. Perhaps this is my gift... Is that why I could see so vividly? Was this possible? Is this a gift? A curse? [God has blessed you eternally.]

Her grandmother's words echoed. "You are not bound to your skin."

"Not bound to my skin," she whispered.

Astrid picked up a photo of her grandmother on her desk, "Is that what you meant?"

She stared at the picture intensely and tears filled her eyes. Something inside hoped she would hear a voice call back to her. Her stare was broken by the lights of the fire engines getting ready to leave the fields across her house.

Her phone suddenly buzzed and a photo of Benny appeared.

It's 1:34 in the morning!

Astrid swiped and answered her video call. "Are you OK?" Even with the not-so-perfect internet connection (what does one expect from spotty phone service in the butt-crack of Texas), it was clear that Benny's eyes were a fiery red and still very wet.

"Girl," he is bawling now. Uncontrollable.

"What's wrong?"

"My mom, dude. My freaking mom. She had a crap attack when I told her I had met with you and your mother earlier."

"Why?"

"I already told you. She says you're a bad influence."

Astrid shook her head. "What's wrong with her?"

"She's a psycho. You know this."

Astrid didn't know what to say. Her mother slapped her, but she didn't think it wise to mention it. No one wants to hear the "I've got it worse than you do," speech when you're having a breakdown. To be honest, Benny's mother was a pill not many people could swallow. None of the Felton's were.

"Benny, I don't know what to say."

"You don't have to say anything, dude. Just know that if I don't reply to your texts anymore, it's because she took my phone. She told me to give my phone to her but I bolted. She's probably going to cancel my service. Dummy probably doesn't know it can work on wifi, though."

"What does your dad say?"

He scoffed. "Absent fathers don't have much of a voice. She said I needed to go to some church near Laredo."

"Gross. What does she want to send you there for?"

"I don't know. She says she's tired of my crap. Honestly, I'm tired of hers, too. I'll be staying with my aunts who have a house over there."

"What about school?"

He exhaled, "I don't know, dude. She wants me gone for a few days. Her royal snooty-ness has banished me. She doesn't want to deal with me."

"That doesn't make any sense."

"You think Regina Felton gives two shits about making sense?"

"Guess not."

He stopped crying. "Whatever. I thought about running away. Maybe going to dad's sister. My Aunt Claire lives in Houston, but she's a psycho, too. Whatever. I prefer to be over there anyway. Anything's better than being here with them," he wiped his eyes dry.

Astrid heard a loud crash coming from outside her door, causing her body to stiffen almost immediately. She instinctively jolted her head towards the door as her mother's face came to mind.

She set the phone down.

"Astrid? What's wrong?" Her heartbeat drummed in her ears, muffling the sound of Benny's voice.

"Mom," she called, but the only audible noises were the rhythmic beeping of the trucks outside and the deep muffled sounds of giant machines tilling the earth. "Momma," she said again from the bedroom door. Her voice trembled.

Another crashing sound and then the sound of her mother screaming. Astrid bolted out of her room so fast she nearly tripped. She had never felt such terror or such a massive pain in her chest. Not even the time she woke up screaming from a nightmare. She dreamt she was flying in the darkness being chased by five angry monsters. Their claws ripping at her ankles. They were about to tear at her foot when her eyes shot open, and she saw her grandmother's face and comforting eyes. She would have preferred one hundred demons to the sound of her mother's terror.

Astrid opened Sarah's bedroom door and saw the lights from the fire trucks pierce through the curtains, giving the room a horrible red and yellow tinge. "Momma," she panted heavily. "Are you alright?"

She flung the door open and felt the dryness of her mouth cut her words. The terror grew. She knew what was coming. Astrid inched her way inside, a malodorous stench penetrated the room. It was like sulfur, only much worse. It was more than the smell of rotten eggs. Something revolting, like the time she found a dead cat by the side of her house. She smelled it even before she saw the rotting cat with its open, twisted black mouth. It was the putrid scent of dead flesh. "Momma," she wailed as she felt a wet warmth on the soles of her bare feet. Astrid looked down and gasped. It was blood. Her mother's blood!

The nightstand had been toppled. Sarah was writhing in a thick black pool of dark matter. Her pajamas were red and black now, her face pale and empty. Sarah lifted herself in manic jerks. "Don't," she extended her arm. Astrid instinctively tried to reach out for her.

"No," growled Sarah. It was a horrible sound, like a wounded animal fighting death. She looked like a white tigress drenched in blood after a poacher's attack. Vocal cords gnarling. Visceral pain. "Don't touch it!"

Astrid stood in shock. She should have immediately reached for the telephone; perhaps an EMT could have revived her mother. Or maybe she could have screamed, opened a window and flagged the firemen and workers across the field. They had a fire truck; the workers could speed through traffic and get her to a hospital fast. But Astrid couldn't do a thing; her body was stoic, fixed, and helplessly rooted to the ground. Only her hands trembled.

"Back—stay back," Sarah choked on hoarse coughs and strained breaths. Black and red chunks and bubbles oozed out of her mouth. She reached for her ankle in pain.

"Momma!" her voice erupted. "What happened?"

She pointed towards an open window in her room.

Astrid reached for her mother's hands. "Don't touch it!" Her ankle had swollen to twice its size and was an angry red color.

Sarah looked at her swollen ankle in defeat. "I did the best I could." Seconds later, her mother's head collapsed on the floor.

"What do you mean? Mom. Mamma!"

Sarah's forehead was drenched in sweat beads. She stared at Astrid with bloodshot eyes as she reached for her.

"Momma," she fell to the ground, wiping the wet strands of hair from her forehead. "Mom," cried Astrid.

"Ride the wind, my beautiful girl," said Sarah as she drifted off into an eternal sleep.

The Devil's Back in Town

I
F I OPEN MY EYES I will cry. I don't want to shed any more tears. Do you understand how painful this is? Do you understand this loneliness? I'm no longer part of a family. I don't have a mother, and I never had a father. I am Astrid, alone.

I'm trying hard not to scream. I want to break out. Out. Yes, because I am very much trapped. I want to run away. Far. Far. Far. As far as far can get. I'd like amnesia most of all. I want to forget. A scream lives inside of me. A big one. It wants to break loose. I'm afraid this anger wants to escape more than I do.

Why is waking up so painful?

Am I awake? No. Perhaps that isn't the right word. Conscious. I am conscious. I feel things now. I used to only see and hear in dreams. I can smell food being cooked here and now. The smoothness of the bed sheets on my forearm and legs is comforting. My eyes are not open, and I certainly can't move my hands. Perhaps my fingers will move a bit. No? Nothing yet. There are voices, muffled at first and then closer, much closer. I feel as though I've been laid on an operating table, and the light is blinding, but there is nothing in the world I can do to open my eyes. The doctors are inspecting me. At least that's what it feels like, but I know better. I'm in my bedroom. I sense people around me. It's been a few days since everything went downhill. Since... Well...

"Ssssttttrrr," the deep, muffled sounds of a woman. "Sssahhh esss sshheeeee poss lllaaaall." Almost, but not quite. A clamor of sounds echoed in the corners of Astrid's mind.

I don't want to die, but I certainly don't want to live. I'm in that in-between place where Hope and Now are two worlds apart. What will become of me? What's left to do if you are not here?

The sound of commotion is coming from below. The clanking of silverware and the moving of chairs. Arguing again. The scent of eggs and chorizo pervaded the air. The scent of store-bought tortillas. How can anyone eat at a time like this?

To be perfectly honest, I don't want to be awake. Is this wrong? To prefer the dream. Even though I have seen vivid and scary things. There's no place I'd rather be than outside my body. My mother would slap me for saying that. I want to slap myself. I have the luxury of life, and I can't imagine waking up. Why is this so painful? I am stuck, like my body is made of metal. A heavy steel weighing me down, suffocating my insides. Just crush me already.

Becoming Astrid was harder and harder. The body was there, but she was still trying to crawl back into reality. Suddenly, her eyes parted open, like when Moses stretched out his hands and the Red Sea divided. Only forms could be seen, as if a thick film grew around her eyes. That was the worst, the feeling of detachment. She longed to be grounded. Colors ran together more and more as if dreams and consciousness were a blurry, fluid canvas. She slipped into both states without truly experiencing either. *Mom. I need my mom,* she thought. She had never felt so helpless and grim.

Now she was looking through her physical eyes, not her mind's eye. This was a real situation. This was a bleak reality, and the images were clear: it was morning, and it had been three days since her mother left this world. Was it a Wednesday? Yes, because the day before was Tuesday, and she had helped pick a coffin on Monday. The funeral home was familiar. It was the same place she said goodbye to her grandmother seven years ago.

Her head struggled to turn. Lights flooded her small room. The yellow on her walls lost its luster as she panned towards her bedroom door and saw the intimidating silhouette of a man and a much smaller woman with unusually wide hips. It was her aunt Sofia and her husband, Hector.

Sofia, with her sour face and peppered gray hair, was the first to enter her room. Her fat husband, with his sun-baked face and wandering eyes followed. As Astrid's mind cleared the fog of unconsciousness, she remembered she hated them, and they hated her.

"Wake up," snarled Sofia, who smelled of cigarette smoke. She poked Astrid's forearm. *"Levantate ya,"* Sofia nudged her husband, "You'd think she was on drugs. I don't understand what's going on with her." Sofia's words were clearer now. Astrid discerned the malice in her voice as she looked up.

My mom just died! That's what's wrong with me! Her heart drummed faster, her mouth was bone dry.

Astrid turned away from her aunt and remembered a dream she had earlier that morning. It was a dream, wasn't it? It seemed real, but the colors she saw were too vivid, almost liquid. In the dream, Astrid was in her living room and could see her aunts and uncles. Her aunts, Sofia and Julia, were sitting at her kitchen table, but their eyes never met.

Julia and Sofia were sisters, but there was nothing familiar about them. They were polar opposites in every way. The only thing binding them was their last name and the pinched, sour faces they bore. They were sisters, but no real connection existed. The Cortezes were a disconnected family, and no amount of good will could rectify this family's union. Hector stood behind Sofia, placing his hands on her shoulders. Astrid never liked Hector; he was always too condescending for his own good. Someone with his lack of education had no business talking down to anyone.

Hector was a stocky man, something akin to a brown bear/rhinoceros hybrid in appearance. But for all of his physical prowess, he was a sheep in wolf's clothing, a hyper-masculine ball of insecurities. An electric bulb pretending to be the sun. He towered over Sofia, but everyone knew she pulled the strings in their marriage. Astrid couldn't remember a time when she didn't feel uncomfortable around her uncle. He wasn't pervy; that wasn't the issue, it was more of a repugnance by default. Unwarranted arrogance leaves a stench that does not wash away. By all accounts, the man appeared to be a decent human. Hector worked hard and was generally away most of the time up in Central Texas, where he worked in the oil rigs. He was simple, he was quiet, and he protected his foul wife with the full range of a mother lion protecting her cubs. If you're going to be as nasty as someone like Sofia, it's best to have a living Minotaur around to make sure other people get attacked instead of you. Ultimately, Uncle Hector was a Keller, and Astrid's grandmother always commented that the Keller's were hateful people. Her grandmother was never wrong.

In the dream, Hector asked if Sarah had any savings.

"Yes," nodded Sofia. "We need Astrid to sign the papers. I think she can. But it's not that much. What is the girl going to live off of?"

"She's almost eighteen," barked Julia. She resembled Sofia, but possessed more pronounced jowls and a thinner frame. Her hair was painted bright red and very short, but the gray at her temples made her scalp look orange. Julia was the eldest and thought of herself as a leader to a flock she never looked after. "She has to start working. She's old enough."

Sofia shook her head. "And what about this house? She has to live somewhere?"

Hector spoke up: "We can sell the house."

"What do you mean?" argued Julia. "You shouldn't even have a say in this. This is my mother's house. It should come back to me. I'm the oldest."

Sofia raised her hand dismissively. "She can stay here until she leaves for college. What will people say if we put the house up right away? They say she's smart. Get her to a college. And keep your voice down, Julia," spat Sofia. "You don't think she can hear you?"

Julia ignored the remark, "She's going to end up crazier than her mother. Didn't you hear her screaming at the hospital? She's not right. *No quedan bien.* Better to kick her out before she does something stupid and burns the house down. You can't tell with people like her."

"Like her?" asked Sofia.

"Yes. You know that's why mom preferred her and Sarah. *Las consentidas.* They did their little tricks together. They're in on it. That *brujeria* trash they do. No-no-no. Mom wasn't right in the head, either. We're going to have to call a priest as soon as we can to clean this place up. Maybe we can ask the Feltons if they want to buy it. It's close to their land. They have just as much reason to want to get her out of here as we do."

Hector asked, "Why are the Feltons concerned about her staying here? What does this have to do with them?"

Julia shook her head haughtily. "Regina told me what Astrid did to her son."

"*Que?* What did Astrid do to Benny?" asked Sofia.

Julia raised her eyebrows high as if to say, "Oh, you know…"

"What?" snapped Sophia. "Spit it out."

"She turned him…" she raised her eyebrows even higher.

"Into a *maricon*," whispered Julia.

"A *maricon?*" repeated Sofia, somewhat bewildered.

Hector crossed his heavy arms. "What?"

Julia raised her arms. "Regina didn't call him that word, but she meant it. She called him 'confused,' but we all know what she means. She was saying something about bad energies and magic. *Pobresita*. To have everything she has and to end up with an embarrassment like that. I'd rather live a simple life than have to deal with something so unnatural. I'm sure Regina would jump at the chance of buying her out of this house. She told me she's going to send the boy off to some church to cure him. It's close by—about two hours away—near Laredo. She called them and they came to her house and everything. She's been planning this for a while, and now I am more than sure she will do it. I'm also sure she won't want Astrid back here when he gets fixed. I think she encourages him. She's just as messed up in the head as he is. Did you hear her last night? Screaming. The way she yelled and then didn't move. It looked like she was dead."

Sofia rolled her eyes. "And what about the father?"

"I don't know what the father thinks of his boy. I'm sure he isn't too thrilled that his son is a *maricon*."

"Not Benny's father," Julia snapped. "I don't give a damn about the gay Felton boy. I meant Astrid's father."

All eyes in the room grew curious.

"The father," grunted Sofia, who quickly laughed into her coffee cup. "The things you say. No. No. We'll think of something, but no need to bring that tornado back into the picture. And keep your voice down. This house has thin walls."

But Astrid heard everything. Every single word. Astrid's body may not have been in the room, but she could see them as easily as she could see the sun outside and empty fields outside. She saw them during her dreams, and

81

she remembered everything they said. They were dreams, weren't they? It's hard to distinguish between fantasy and reality these days. It was different, though. It was a different sight. A dream-like sight she couldn't understand.

Back in her room, Astrid was still lying in bed and suddenly tasted blood. She hated feeling trapped in her body. It was still heavy, and her lungs struggled to breathe.

Aunt Sofia leaned in, "We heard you're crying and screaming." A casual observer may have heard those words and been convinced of her sincerity. But only Astrid was able to observe Sofia's face and the way she sneered. Her family had the inherent ability to always make her feel like dirt.

The heavy-set silhouette of her uncle appeared next to Sofia. "I don't want you to get upset," Hector whispered, turning towards the door. "Don't make a scene." He leaned into her ear. "Your sister is here."

"Don't be stupid. I know that, I was just talking to her–"

"—Not Julia," he said, his eyes widened. "The other one."

"What?!" Sofia's face turned pale, and her eyes widened. "Who called her? What is she doing here?"

A shadow appeared at the foot of Astrid's bed. Astrid remembered the voice instantly. It was her aunt, Marianne.

Marianne Cortez wasn't part of the equation. She hadn't been for quite some time. She left the family over seven years ago, about the time her grandma Carmen passed. Astrid was uneasy seeing Marianne at the foot of her bed, wearing a short black skirt and a frilly charcoal top. Astrid hadn't realized what a striking resemblance her aunt bore to her mother. She knew she was awake. She felt the tightness of her throat and the pain in her jaw (she clenched them when she slept), but she wondered if her mind was playing tricks on her—perhaps this was still one of her dreams.

"Wake up, Kid," said the forgotten, husky voice. Marianne sat next to Astrid and said, "The Devil's back in town."

The Strange, Estranged Sister

S
T. MARY'S CATHOLIC Church appeared gray under the cloudy December sky. Despite the drear, the building brought Astrid some consolation. She recalled attending mass with her grandmother, sitting next to older people in the middle of the pews whose names she could no longer remember.

Astrid staggered towards the front of the church as strangers extended their hands. All of them hugged her and offered condolences. A tender kiss touched her from an old woman she had never met. Perhaps she was one of her grandmother's friends. "You're in my thoughts," the *senora* said in Spanish.

Benny sat next to his mom, Regina, on the right side of the pews. The tall, unattractive woman with a sour face was the perfect funeral attendee. Though Regina knew she wouldn't win any beauty contests, she considered herself a community pillar. Lifting her eyebrows was an art for her, almost like an Olympic sport at which she was a gold medalist. Regina painted her sparse arches with precision and let them fly high when she entered a room. She scanned. She ranked. Regina smiled when they smiled, but the eyebrows remained at attention. She was a Felton, and the Felton's built the town of Diller. Not Anglo by birth, Regina was fair-skinned and didn't have a Tex-Mex accent. If she was careful, she even faked a twang that most thought genuine. Benny never missed an opportunity to smack her back into reality. Her son would often mock her when they were alone in their car. "You know your last name is Rodriguez, right?"

"Only when it's convenient." His mother pressed her lips to the side and snidely replied. Benny didn't understand what she meant until Regina reminded him that his senior year was around the corner and universities had quotas. "You don't have the best grades, Benny. It might look better if you call yourself Benjamin Felton-Rodriguez. You know, in case you need to use that golden ticket. If it works for those people, it can work for you too."

Regina hugged him, comforting the visibly upset boy. Even though Benny looked like a ferret coiled up by a pale cobra, it was still a moving sight. When he turned and met with Astrid's heavy, red glare, his face erupted into tears. He was about to stand up when Regina reached for his hand and squeezed it hard.

Astrid gave Benny an "It's fine, don't worry about it" nod and walked down the church until sitting in the second row, behind her two aunts. "Sit there and don't make a scene," said Sofia. "*Calladita.*"

It's incredible how these people, these two absent women, could have such authority over my life, thought Astrid. *I never understood my history teachers until now: totalitarian governments. Our government was overthrown by a violent coup. And I don't even have my best friend with me. No one. It should be me in the coffin.*

Astrid was about to cry again when she heard the echo of heels hitting a cold floor. Who knows why she didn't take off her sunglasses, but there she was, Marianne Cortez in all of her I will-never-will-look-over-forty glory. The strange, estranged sister. The one who ordered Astrid out of bed not more than an hour ago, stood in a tight black dress and the reddest lipstick Astrid had ever seen. Her body let off a sexual magnetism that married men crave. It made the women's eyes become thin slits of rage. For the first time in three days, she felt a smile forming. Astrid didn't know very much about her aunt, but she loved seeing what her presence was doing to the Pinched Sisters. Marianne sat in the first row on the left side of the church, crossed her legs, and didn't move as people tried to console her.

Marianne's so strange, thought Astrid. *I wish I was cold like her. She's actively avoiding people and probably hasn't even shed a tear. Why would she? We haven't heard from her in so long. Can you cry for someone you don't even know anymore? It's been seven years, and people change.* She shook her head, then lowered it. *What the hell will I do now?* She asked herself the question over and over. It had become one long word which carried a weight and a sadness she had never felt. *This wasn't supposed to happen. Not at all. Mom was healthy. So vibrant.* She couldn't understand why the doctors had been so callous. How insane they sounded.

She played the unbelievable scene over and over in her mind's eye. A doctor told both Julia and Astrid that Sarah was "very sick" and "there was nothing we could do about it." The cancer had spread. *What cancer? What is he talking about? Momma wasn't even sick.* "It probably started in the kidney and spread rapidly. No stopping it after it hits the kidneys, I'm afraid. The blood. It filters the blood, you know. And where does the blood go?" *She was healthy! What do you mean it started in the kidneys?*

"Everywhere," Julia shook her head. "It goes everywhere. And fast. *Se desparamo.*"

He was really just talking to Julia when he said, "We found fluid in your sister's lungs." She heard his words echo in her head. "The cancer is in her lungs, in her liver, and in her kidneys. Her airways are blocked by a substantial number of tumors. We have her sedated right now." The doctor showed her an x-ray and pointed to several white spots over her mother's lungs. *This can't be real!* "I can't explain how anyone could have missed this. " He looked at her and very calmly said, "I'm afraid she's not going to make it." The tall doctor with a large nose talked casually about cancer. Monotonous. As if it were a head cold or a fever blister. Nothing benign at all. Something to be taken care of with a simple trip to CVS. And the way that it spread. What a nice little fairy story. *How can someone suddenly develop cancer? How could we not know? She was never even sick! She was fine! Not a bump, not a single symptom. She never even touched a cigarette! The Pinched Sisters were the ones who smoked like chimneys in winter! Something like cancer doesn't spread to vital organs so fast. It's a load of crap. I don't believe it for one minute.*

A sudden murmur shattered her thoughts. Astrid could hear whispers from the rows behind her: "I don't know why God does these things." She turned back to see her neighbors, Isabel and Tomasa. The elderly widowed sisters shared the little pink house at the edge of Astrid's neighborhood. They were paper-thin in both appearance and personality with a constant scowl chiseled across their withering, aged faces.

"How did she die?" asked Tomasa. "She was so young, wasn't she the same age as your daughter, Hilda? Didn't they graduate together?"

"No, Tomasa. My Hilda was older. Closer in age to Julia. I think Sarah was in her early forties."

"*Tan joven!* So young!"

"*No me canso de decirle a mi* Roberto to be careful when he's working in the rigs. Bumps and accidents are dangerous. They become cancerous if you are not careful. You don't feel anything for a while, but something begins to grow inside you without you even realizing it. They said she had tumors everywhere. *Pobresita.* In the liver. In the lungs. They don't know how it started. I overheard Julia earlier. It was eating her from the inside out, and she didn't even know it."

"*Dios mio!*" She made the sign of the cross.

"Poor thing," said Tomasa. "You think she may have gotten them because he used to beat her."

"Who?"

"*El Gringo.* That ex-husband of hers. He was a drunkard. I remember Carmencita would cry during our prayer group and tell us how worried she was about Sarah. We prayed for her every week. I don't remember his name. I don't even know how they met," she sighed. "But I always wanted to ask Carmen why she didn't tell her daughter that the man she married was going to ruin her. If she was as good as people said she was, then all of this could have been avoided. Some card reader she turned out to be."

"I had no idea," she replied.

"Yes. It was a *mugrero.* Sarah moved in with Carmen, and Adam followed her. I think that was his name. They called the police one night because he went inside the house and wanted to steal the baby. He had already hit Sarah when the police found him. Her face was unrecognizable. I saw it myself! I don't know how they managed to talk to the *Gringo,* but he let the baby go. Only God knows where he is now." She paused for a moment. "He probably gave her that damned disease because of all those hits. Poor thing. Some women were brought here only to suffer."

Astrid's face burned red, she felt maddening rage within her. She had never heard anything so vile. Could the words of these old crows be true? No one told her much about her father, only that he left when Astrid was born. It didn't bother her. Astrid preferred not to know anything about him anyway. She was proud of being raised by women. *Down with the Patriarchy.* But why did those two old bags know more than she did about the matter? What else wasn't she aware of? Did she even want to know? *Can you be an orphan if one of your parents is still alive? Is he alive?* The thoughts raged on.

Astrid wanted to explode, to erase herself and everything around her. To fly like her great-great-grandmother—away. To escape the horror of her mother's last breath, escape the terrible story she heard. Everything. She wanted it to end.

Was it wrong to avoid the coffin? It was closed either way. Astrid knew her mother wasn't there anymore. She couldn't feel her spirit.

The emptiness wasn't there when Sarah collapsed into her own blood, or when Astrid ran towards the fields across her home screaming at a group of firemen. No, the emptiness happened while she was crying on the ground in the middle of the smoky sugarcane field. Astrid was inconsolable, surrounded by a crowd when she suddenly stopped. Everything went eerily still when she turned back towards her small, two-story home. That's when Astrid felt it. A frigid pierce through her heart. *Something turned off.*

The Pinched Sisters didn't let Astrid see the body at the funeral home, but that was perfectly fine. She didn't want to remember her mother that way, bloodless, hollow and pale. Sarah looked alive and well the night of her death. She didn't understand why people were saying cancer had taken her. How could that be? It was something else. It had to be! Her mother was fine, laughing and bantering with her even on the night it happened. How could she have something as terrible and life-draining as cancer and not know? With the number of tumors they said she had, wouldn't they have found out sooner? Surely her mother would have been in worse shape. She would have lost weight. Lost her appetite. Her hair. Something! You don't act fine one day and vomit blood the next. Something was not right. She didn't accept this insane diagnosis. It was wrong. Astrid was sure of this. Deep down in her heart, she knew that something was not right.

Her Uncle Hector suddenly turned around to face her, and with one of his trademark scornful smiles whispered, "Where's your camera now?" He sniggered. "Don't you want to take a picture?" he motioned towards the coffin. Astrid felt her face turn red.

A small, rotund priest suddenly appeared on the altar. "We are gathered in our father's house to mourn the memory of Sarah Cortez," he began. "Who was taken from us this week by a silent and malicious poison. Cancer, a cancer that grew. Cancer that was undetected and abrupt. And what is cancer? Cancer is the—"

"—It wasn't cancer," Astrid hissed under her breath.

She glanced at Marianne and could tell that her aunt was rolling her eyes behind those thick, dark glasses of hers.

"Cancer is a curse on the body. It is never easy to say goodbye to our loved ones," persisted the priest. "She leaves behind sisters and a daughter. Our beloved Sarah was taken from us at such a young age. This reminds us of the fragility of life, how utterly, utterly precious it is. How the things we take for granted, the simple pleasures of life can be taken in the blink of an eye. A body, once alive and thriving, can succumb to the ravages of disease. The wages of sin is death, and only through Christ can we achieve everlasting life. We hear a lot about cancer–"

Astrid's tone gained in volume as she uttered involuntarily, "It wasn't cancer!"

Her outburst frightened those behind her, causing Marianne to turn her head towards her. The priest cleared his throat. "Which is a horrible, horrible disease. Cancer has taken—"

"It wasn't cancer," Astrid shot up. "Stop calling it CANCER! It wasn't cancer!" The two old ladies behind her shifted back, alarmed by the outburst. A shrewd smile formed across Marianne's stoney face.

The priest fell silent, almost dropping his microphone. "I'm sorry," he said nervously, staring at Astrid in a way that one would look at an intruder.

"It wasn't cancer!" Astrid repeated, louder and aggressively. "She didn't have FUCKING cancer! She never had any Goddamned CANCER!" She was screaming at this point, but she didn't care. Not one bit.

Sofia leapt to her feet. She looked like one of those jack-in-the-box toys. "Astrid!"

Hector was leaning against the pew as well, ready to yell. Julia was shaken as well, but she pinched her lips because she wouldn't cause a scene in public. Sofia bit her tongue and clenched her jaw. Even Isabel and Tomasa had their arms across their chests. The only audible sound was the broken and light laughter coming from her aunt Marianne.

Sofia banged her hands on the pew. "What is wrong with you! Have some respect, girl. You're in God's house. Have some respect. For the sake of your mother!" She covered her mouth with a handkerchief. Hector stood up, laying his arms around her shoulders. He shook his head at Astrid then looked away.

Astrid could hardly see anyone anymore. Her eyes were so full of tears. "But he's lying. She was fine." She repeated it much softer, but she didn't think anyone heard her. She turned to Marianne, but her eyes remained fixed on the coffin.

"He... he's lying. She never—she never—" Astrid's voice drifted. She couldn't take it anymore, the angry eyes were too much for her. The people gasped as Astrid shot out of the church.

"The girl is upset," insisted the priest. "She's lost her mother. We cannot all come to grips with what the Lord commands." She could hear the priest above the murmurings. "Please. Let us continue. Let us continue honoring the memory of Susana—"

There was an audible gasp followed by murmuring throughout the church. The priest glanced at his notes. His eyes widened when he realized the mistake. "Sarah. Forgive me," he mumbled. "The girl's outburst," his voice trailed as he attempted to correct his slip-up. The priest felt his cheeks flush. "Sarah. Our beloved Sarah Cortez."

Something Turned Off

ASTRID HIT THE PAVEMENT with force. Something propelled her out of the church. She had to leave the lies spewing out of the priest's mouth and get away from the Pinched Sisters. In a perfect world, Benny would have bolted out of there with her. But she was running alone, crying harder than she ever had. Would her mother have been ashamed of her outburst? Would she have even cared? Or would she have wryly said, "I told you you were full of drama." She didn't know. All she knew was her feet were taking her towards the lonely cemetery at the end of town. To the place where they would lay her mother's bones.

Men had already gathered at the gravesite. They wore white shirts and sunglasses and stared sympathetically as she looked at the large hole. She stood there for a moment, catching her breath, before one of the men asked her if she needed anything. "No," she whispered, then walked towards a grave slab nearby. She didn't want to be near the hole.

What am I going to do?

Her eyes trembled.

What am I going to do, mom?

She suddenly heard a crack. Was that the sound of death? Was the end coming for her, too? It wouldn't surprise her. Nothing surprised her anymore. A shadow suddenly appeared behind a grave house next to her.

"You were always such a drama queen," said Marianne. "Even as a child." A part of Astrid was relieved to see her aunt. Her face, stoic as it was, resembled her mother's. It gave her some comfort knowing Marianne hated her family as much as she did.

"How did you get here?"

"Same way you did, kid." She sat on a grave slab beside Astrid.

"Apparently, we're all dramatic," replied Astrid, "It's in the blood. Nothing to be done about it."

"You alright, kid?"

The question gave her pause. No one had asked her how she felt. You'd think it would be a question she would be getting from everyone, but no one had bothered to ask her how she was handling this tragedy. How was she coping with the death of her mother? But then again, what would they expect her to say? "I'm on the verge of a nervous breakdown," is what Astrid would want to say. But most people would want to hear her say, "I'm fine. She'd want me to survive." Most people don't want to listen to the truth. It's like cyanide to them. Astrid could tell Marianne was not like most people, so she said: "I'm thinking about jumping into that hole." Astrid pointed to her mother's final resting place.

Marianne nodded, her lips curling up as if to say, "I hear you," but then proceeded to give a quick laugh. "Sarah was right about you!"

"What's that supposed to mean? Why are you laughing at me? Can't you see I'm in pain?"

"Sassy. She said you're full of sass. I'm not laughing at you. I'm laughing at the pickle you are in," she clicked her tongue. "Well, that's the pickle we are in."

"You?" Astrid scoffed. "You didn't lose your mother. You have no idea what I'm feeling. You sashay back into our lives with those stupid sunglasses and this cold attitude, and you think you know what any of us are feeling." Astrid tried to see past the thick plastic of her dark shades. She needed to see her aunt's eyes. What was hiding behind them? Why was she here? Why was she so callous?

"I knew your mother way before you did. She's been my best friend for over 39 years. I've known her twice as long as you have. Don't tell me I don't know what you're feeling. She may not have been my mother, but she was my sister. We share a history you will never know."

"I didn't even know she talked to you."

Mariana sneered. "There's a lot you don't know about your mother, kid. Or yourself for that matter," she paused for a moment then tapped on the grave slab. "Do you know who we are sitting on?" she asked suddenly.

Astrid read the inscription on the black slab. "It says Narcissa Mendez, A Beloved Mother."

Marianne pulled out and lit a cigarette from her red purse.

"Mother-yes. Beloved-hell no. She was a snake."

Astrid's face snapped back, almost offended. "She's dead."

Marianne inhaled the smoke. "Good. The world is full of enough snakes. Like your stupid aunts. What a waste of life."

"You knew this woman, Narcissa Mendez?"

She nodded in disgust. "Yeap. This old bag used to scream at your mother and I on our way to school. Told us she didn't want us anywhere near her boys. She didn't even want them walking next to us on our way home from school. She would stand outside her crappy little house and tell them to stay away from us. We were bad people." She turned to Astrid. "As if your mother and I would look twice at her miscreants."

"Why didn't she like you?"

"Because we were better than her. Isn't that the real reason people hate each other? While they won't admit it, it's right there: jealousy. It's disguised, of course, but this old hag really wanted what we had," she exhaled.

"What did she want?"

"She wanted to be like us, to have our gifts. Before she found Jesus, she always asked momma for card readings and spells to hook that lowlife she married. After she got what she wanted, she never returned to the house and started badmouthing us when her husband cheated on her. Well, how was momma supposed to put a stop to his wandering pecker? It was half his personality! She'd have to turn him into a vegetable to keep him from cheating again."

"Poor lady."

"Poor lady, my ass. That *pendeja* deserved it. No one told her to go around trying to catch a cheater. Magic is only good when it comes on its own. She didn't want a husband. She wanted a puppet. But the puppet walked away.

She never forgave momma."

A group of mourners walked along the path from the church to the cemetery behind a hearse carrying Sarah's coffin. Astrid remembered being in a similar line when her grandmother passed away.

"Why are you here?" asked Astrid.

"That's a stupid question," she said softly.

"I haven't seen you in years. You have never once visited."

Marianne looked away. "I had no reason to come visiting until a few days ago."

"Who told you about momma? I know aunt Sofia and aunt Julia didn't tell you. It's obvious they hate you. How'd you find out about any of this?"

She shook her head. "Called?" Marianne scoffed. "No one called me, kid."

"Then how did you find out about my mom?"

Marianne was quiet for a moment. "Something inside me turned off."

Listening to Marianne gave Astrid a sense of comfort. It wasn't that her aunt looked like her mother. She almost resonated with a similar energy. Astrid knew exactly what Marianne was talking about because she also felt something "turn off" after her mother died. This was a bond, a deep and primitive bond which Astrid was beginning to form with her estranged aunt.

Astrid rested her head against Marianne's shoulder; she knew they shared this truth. Marianne wrapped her left arm around Astrid as a tear fell from behind her aunt's thick sunglasses.

Mourners had made their way into the cemetery when Astrid spotted the Pinched Sisters. Even from a distance, their gaze was piercing at her. She followed Julia as she marched toward them.

"Well, I hope you're happy with the spectacle you made of yourself," barked Julia. "Get off of there! Both of you are so disrespectful. Smoking! At a cemetery? Are you kidding me?"

They were still sitting on Narcissa's gravestone. Astrid looked for a sign from Marianne. Was she going to cave in? Or was she as stubborn and mean-spirited as everyone claimed? Marianne lowered her head to the ground, shaking it lightly.

"Why did you do that, Astrid? *Que verguenza.*" Her face shifted towards

Julia's. Astrid never noticed how ugly her aunt was. Even under the cloudy sky, she could see time was not on her side. The bags under her eyes were heavy, and her cheeks had folded over ever since the doctor insisted Julia lose weight or surrender to a diabetic future. There were thick skin tags around her neck, which she covered with fake pearls. "What's wrong with you?" she pressed, "You can't talk to a priest like that! Have you gone crazy! Crazy like her." She pointed at Marianne.

"Leave me alone," said Astrid. She didn't want to look at her pinched face anymore.

Rage took over Julia. "Who the hell do you think you are?" She gripped Astrid's arm and sank her nails into her flesh, making Astrid's body cringe. It all happened so quickly, she didn't even have time to scream.

Marianne instinctively reached for Julia's forearm. Julia's forearm muscles began rising, wriggling and twisting under her creepy skin. She let out a painful growl. The smell of sulfur filled the air, a carnelian-colored handprint formed on Julia's arm. "You know better than that," snarled Marianne.

Julia cupped her forearm and shook her head. "God damn you," she spat in disbelief, staring at her throbbing arm. "Why did you come back here? Why the hell can't you just leave us alone?" Julia fumed, her body stiffening as she faced Astrid. "It was you, wasn't it? You called her, didn't you?" Julia's eyes, aflame with anger, bore into Astrid. "You stupid girl," she shrieked almost maniacally. "You don't even know what you've done."

Astrid didn't understand.

Julia shook her head. "You brought the devil back here."

Marianne shrugged with a creepy, crooked smile.

A LIGHT RAIN FELL on the funeral. Marianne opened her umbrella, pulling Astrid close while she held it above them. Astrid looked at Marianne's hand with some trepidation. What was this strange power she had? She burned Tia

Julia's skin, she saw it with her own eyes. The way her muscles spasmed was disgusting. And why did she smell that horrible stench when it happened?

One of the pallbearers almost slipped while setting the casket lowering device. The twelve chairs under the blue tent were quickly filled by the eldest and fattest members of the mourners. Marianne and Astrid stood together in the back of the tent. Astrid noticed Julia animatedly rubbing her arm, as if recalling the earlier experience. Sofia shook her head and crossed her arms.

When the family was instructed to throw dirt on the coffin, Astrid declined. Marianne didn't throw anything either. There was no reason to perform—that's what all of this was anyway, just one elaborate performance. She knew her mother wasn't here anymore. Her body would be in the ground very soon, and in time her flesh would decay, and her bones would be all that was left. Her shell, that's what it was, after all, would disappear. But Astrid also knew a part of her mother would never truly leave. They had several conversations and she remembered them well: "You will hear me in death," Sarah once said.

"Don't get scared when I come back and pull your feet at night. Don't cause a scene."

"You're going to come up from Hell just to scare me?"

"No, heathen, I'm going to float my pearly ass down from the gates of Heaven, hide under your bed and reach for your ankles when you get up from bed. I'd fight time and space to come back just to bother you."

"That's a sick thought, mom."

"It's not sick. It's instinct. You think you're going to get rid of me when I'm gone?" She reached out and hugged Astrid. "I'll come back to scare and criticize my little baby," she laughed.

"Something to look forward to, I guess."

Sarah kissed Astrid's cheek. "I'll be back," Sarah used a cheesy Arnold Schwarzenegger voice. "Don't worry. You'll hear my voice again. Just wait."

Back at the Diller Catholic Cemetery, three men began to dig at the pile of earth and fill the grave as tears streamed down Astrid's face. "I'm waiting for your voice," she whispered.

Only Marianne could hear her words.

Astrid froze when her aunt said: "Soon."

95

Marianne and Astrid

MARIANNE AND ASTRID sat in the Cortez living room after the funeral. Astrid's gaze settled on one of her mother's pink romance novels. I need to escape into one of those sappy, silly plots, she mused. The ride from the cemetery to their home had been silent, making the journey feel much longer than it was.

Marianne had maintained an upright posture, seemingly searching for the right moment to start their conversation. But she slumped back into the loveseat after Astrid's distant expression persisted. "I know you probably don't want to talk about your mother. I understand," she said, reaching for a cigarette from her purse. She lit it before Astrid could voice her aversion to the smell. "If I were in your shoes, I probably wouldn't want to discuss it either."

With her arms crossed, Marianne looked on as a tear slid down Astrid's cheek. "I wish Benny were here. He's stronger than I am."

"Why do I know that name? I've heard it before. I think your mother used to mention his name."

"Benny is my best friend."

Marianne inhaled a thick puff of smoke. "Since you don't want to talk about Sarah. Why don't you tell me about him?"

"He's hilarious. He's got blue hair. He's my gay best friend." She smiled effervescently. "I like his confidence. Benny has the privilege of being white and coming from money. It's easy to be an idealist when your life is ideal."

"High praise. You make this kid sound like a Kennedy."

"No," she scoffed. "Benny lives down the road. He's not actually white. He's half white. Benny. Benny Felton."

Marianne cringed. "A Felton is your best friend?"

"Yes. We've known each other all our lives."

"And this little gay boy with the blue hair is a Felton?" she almost seemed giddy. She tapped the cigarette on an empty plate. Marianne's eyes were wide and beaming. "Is he the skinny little kid I saw at the church at the funeral sitting next to Gina?"

"Yeah. He was next to Regina, his mom. I like his confidence. He's so comfortable in his skin. He feels—"

"—I should have put two and two together," she said louder. "He was sitting right next to Gina. God, I hate that bitch."

A nervous laugh escaped Astrid's lips. "A lot of people don't like her."

"All those people can't be wrong. She's obviously pissed off plenty of people. It's nice to know some things never change," Marianne smirked.

"Why are you suddenly so happy?"

She inhaled again. "Because, Kid, sometimes the world gives you extra dessert. You have to savor it."

"And what's the dessert?"

"That tall and bitter Gina Felton, with her nose in the air and a stick up her ass, has a little fairy flying next to her."

"What's that supposed to mean?"

"Oh, for God's sake, kid, take that stupid "I can't believe you voted Republican" face. I love the gays. But I'll bet you my left tit that Regina Felton doesn't like the fact that our little Bobby has a nice set of sparkly wings."

"Benny!"

"Whatever."

"Yeah, she doesn't like it. Not one bit."

"Tell him not to let that get him down. Regina doesn't like anyone, not even herself. She doesn't even love her own husband."

"How do you know?" asked Astrid

"Sometimes we think we want something. We wish very hard for it, and, to our detriment, we get it. She always loved the idea of Benny's father. Regina wanted a way out of Regina's world and into the Felton world. Regina always wanted to get to the top."

"You think she's at the top?"

"Well, the top can be subjective, kid. In her world, she's at the top. She's got a nice house, which is a big upgrade from her childhood home. She's got a little bit of influence. She's got the Felton name. She always wanted that... I'm sure that's really the only thing she wanted. Gina always did want to erase the stigma of her ethnicity. But that's as far as she's ever going to go. Essentially, it's deplorable because that's all she's ever wanted."

"She always wanted a son. That's what she tells Benny."

"But her son is gay," Marianne gave an exaggerated sigh. "I'm sure she didn't want that. She should have been more specific when praying."

"No. She's sending Benny away."

"Doesn't surprise me. Is she shipping the boy off to the military or something? They've become very lax about the gays."

"No," said Astrid. "She's sending him to a church to get better?"

"Get better?"

"To cure him."

"There's no cure for God's will."

"God's? What's God got to do with this?"

"God made that boy, and God made him gay. Of course, someone with Regina's superiority complex *would* want to go against the will of God."

"She seems like a very sad woman. I don't see her much anymore, but she always looks kind of quiet and kind of mad when I do. Like she's having a conversation with herself."

"That's the face of disillusion, kid. Stay away from people who have that look. They're looking to steal your light because theirs is gone. They'll bring you down with them if you let them."

"So, that's why you don't like her, because she settled."

"I'm not saying that she settled. She won, when you think about it. This is all she ever wanted. I don't like her because she's a nasty person. She's a hateful human being willing to do whatever she wants to get ahead in life. I think what bothers me the most is that the pinnacle of her success is insulting.

I'd have more conviction for her if she actually wanted something greater. I would respect her more if she wanted to rule more than just a dusty town."

"Not everyone has your ambition, Marianne. Not everyone wants to be like the wind."

"The wind?"

"Yeah, that's what Mom used to say about you, that you were like the wind. She said you would come and go. You wanted to see things, and that's why we didn't see you. You're invisible. Like the Wind."

"Your mother was a nice person, but she was really full of crap."

"Rude much," Astrid snapped.

"I don't know what she meant by telling you that, but I am not some avid traveler, kid. I wouldn't say I like to travel, to be perfectly honest. I stayed away for a reason."

"And what reason was that? You can't just get me started and then not tell me something as important as this."

"What I can tell you is that Regina Felton is a nasty lady who you need to stay away from. As far as the Felton boy goes, I don't know what Regina has in store for him with that supposed church, but nothing good ever comes from trying to divert the will of God. The reason I was 'the wind' as your mother poetically described me was for the family benefit." Marianne abruptly left the room.

Astrid realized that Marianne was not willing to elaborate.

Jesus, Mary and Josephine Baker

A S THE EVENING progressed, Astrid's thoughts kept reminiscing on the rage that came from her aunt when she attacked Julia. A dormant rage had awakened, unleashing the smell of sulfur. Why had Marianne said those things about her?

Where was her mother now? Was she resting? Happy? She wanted to hear Sarah's voice; she wanted a sarcastic remark. Her real voice. Not the one that echoed in her mind. A witty remark. The banter of mother and child turned friends.

Friends. The thought echoed inside her head.

She needed a friend. As difficult as it was to admit, she needed Benny. She loved him. This was obvious to her, but she didn't like knowing that she needed a shoulder to cry on right now. But no one was left, except for Marianne. But Marianne was still relatively unknown. A stranger who became stranger with every conversation. She needed familiarity. She needed a diversion.

Benny.

She reached for her cell phone and video-called her one true friend. It took a while, but his face eventually appeared on her phone.

"Hey," he said weakly, looking away from the camera.

"Hey." She didn't know what else to say. What else could she say?

He wasn't himself. His eyes were puffy and his hair was disheveled. It was apparent he had been crying. He was a lesser version of Benny. "Are you alright?"

"I'm supposed to be asking you that."

He started crying.

"Oh, Benny," she said, her eyes wet with tears.

"Jesus, Mary and freaking Josephine Baker," he wiped away tears. "This is why I didn't want to call you. I've been crying non-stop. I can only imagine what you're going through."

She couldn't say anything. Astrid wanted to tell Benny that she was dying inside, but she couldn't. How could she begin to tell him about all the pain? In what way could she convey how confused she felt, or how she wanted to get her mother back and get her life back to the mundane, but sensible existence of before. Astrid couldn't tell Benny about her aunt or the things she could do with her gifts. He'd think she was crazy. She thought she was crazy herself. What she could tell him was that she was lonely, very far from the world, but she wasn't sure he could handle it. Benny was a lovable clown at heart but nothing is sadder than seeing a sad clown.

Benny shook his somber head. Something was wrong with him. It wasn't the haggard appearance. He looked gaunt, and his eyes were sunken. He had obviously been crying, but the hollowness of his soul had permeated onto his exterior. More than sad, the boy looked broken, devoid of hope. Devoid of spirit. He abruptly pushed his hair back and tied it behind his back. Astrid saw the faintest sign of scratches and cuts on his left forearm.

"Did you hurt yourself?" she questioned. "What are those marks?"

He pushed his sleeves down and brushed off the question. "Don't you start, too," he muttered.

Astrid nodded, satisfied with the answer. "You need to be careful," she said.

Benny nodded. "I wish I were there with you," his voice cracked. "I should be there with you."

Astrid's heart broke. She feared all the emotions would end up breaking her heart into tiny shards, a powder of its former self. "Benny, I don't want to think about anything. The only reason I called is to hear the sound of your voice. Just seeing your face gives me some comfort. Comfort is not something I have had at all this week. So you're going to have to calm down, and you're going to have to be stronger because you are my rock for now, and I need my rock to be strong."

Benny cleared his throat and composed himself. "I know most people don't expect me to be a great comfort, so I appreciate you telling me that. The truth of the matter is I'm not very strong. I want you to know, even though I'm easy to break, I put myself together very, very well. It's a gift. I think all gay people have this God-given ability to heal from the inside out. You're one of the reasons I keep putting myself back together. I don't know what I would do if I weren't your friend, and I hate to turn it around, but Benny is Benny. I'm here for you, and I will always be here for you. I want you to know that you will survive this, you dumb slut."

"Ay, Benny." She exhaled heavily after a moment of silence, "Yes, I'll survive." A half-smile formed on her face. "I have to. And thank you for coming to the funeral."

"I wanted to sit with you, you know. During the funeral, I mean. I didn't want you to be alone." He was more composed now.

"I know you did."

"My stupid mother didn't let me go to you," he sighed.

"I knew you would have come if you could've."

"And when I saw you yelling," he started crying again. "At the dumbass priest, I wanted to follow you."

"It's better you didn't. Really."

"You were all alone. And I couldn't be there for you. You're my best friend. You're the bitch I love the most. I let you run out of the church and the people—everyone just started bashing you. I didn't do anything to stop them. Even my mom, dude. She's a piece of work. Don't even get me started on that one."

"What did she say?"

"On our way home, she told me she was sending me away for-sure-for-sure. Like she has these plans for me. I'm leaving for a retreat soon."

"For what?"

"It's a church thing. They're sending me there to get the gay out of me. They don't want me to think evil thoughts, but they don't mind filling me with the body of Christ. Sounds pretty gay to me," he bemused.

Astrid started laughing without realizing it. A deep laugh. The irreverent and inappropriate laughter gave her such pleasure and life for the first time in three days. Laughter echoed through the entire second story of her home. "Oh my God. I needed that."

Benny grinned, "I'm always glad to help."

"Well, they can try to put the holy spirit in you, but I think it's going to be pretty crowded. You're pretty spirited already. But what about school?"

"I don't know," said Benny. "I don't think she's thought this through. I think she's going through some kind of meltdown, to be honest. She's been acting weirder than usual. Everything makes her nervous, and she's really jumpy. She's paranoid about something. I don't know what. I feel like I know her less and less every day. Whatever, not like I'm going to miss out on anything important anyway. I don't think there is anything wrong with me. I don't know why she insists on these ridiculous ideas."

Astrid sighed. "I thought I knew people. But if this week has taught me anything, it's that people don't show you their truth. My granny used to say: *Caras vemos corazones no sabemos.*"

"Yup. We can see a person's face but never their heart. Speaking of faces... who was the lady in the front row? Is she related to you?"

"That's my aunt Marianne. She's another one whose heart we have yet to see."

"Oh, she's the one my mom and your aunts kept talking about; they came here after the burial. They were here for a long time. I even heard your aunt with the red hair-"

"Julia, that's Julia."

"—that one was complaining about that Marianne chick. Apparently, she burned her. It didn't make sense to me. She sounds like a real badass, though. I wasn't really paying attention."

"What else did they say about her?"

"A lot of stuff. Said she ran off with a man a few days after your grandma passed away. Didn't even stay around for the *novenario*. And she was greedy and nothing but bad news. Yeah, they were going on and on about her. I don't think they like her. They didn't say a lot of bad things about you because I was there and they obviously know you're my friend. Do you trust Marianne?"

"She's been supportive, and I can tell she wants to help me. On the other hand, I don't know this woman. I don't know where she's been, and I haven't really sat down and talked to her about it. I think it's weird that she hasn't even mentioned any of this to me. Why do her own sisters hate her so much? I know I shouldn't trust what my aunts say, but hate doesn't happen by accident; it starts somewhere. I'm sure there's some truth to what they say. I don't know. To be honest, I don't know where I stand with her, but for the most part, I'm calmer now that she's here. Again, *caras vemos corazones no sabemos.*"

Astrid wondered whether she should tell him more details, but Benny wasn't the greatest person at giving advice. Benny was the kind of friend you used to forget situations with, not analyze them.

"At least you're not alone."

"No," said Astrid. "No, I'm not alone. But I'm still lonely if that makes any sense."

"I get you. Listen, girl. I have to help my mom. She said some people were coming over tonight. I'm thinking she's having another Bingo Night. They've been cooking *menudo* all day. Maybe it's for Luci. I think she's raising money to help pay for her daughter's surgery."

"That's nice of your mom, but it's a shame we have to crowdsource healthcare. *Pinche* Republicans."

"I know," he scoffed.

"Alright. I'll let you go. I'm pretty sure I'm going to have to start going back to school very soon. I've just been out of it. I'll ask Marianne about it, but I'm not even thinking about going back yet. There are just too many unresolved things we need to finish."

"It's understandable. Try to get some rest, too. I know you're in mourning and all, but you look like hell. Looking like hell is never OK."

Astrid laughed again. "I'll do my best to hide my misery and pretty up for you next time I see you."

"There's that glaring American sense of decency I knew you had. I can't be seen with an ugly hag."

"OK, Benny. Love you."

"Love you more."

She scanned the clock. It was barely six o'clock. Astrid couldn't possibly close her eyes and turn off her mind. Her eyes perked up as she looked outside her window and saw a car driving towards her house.

Malas Caras

THE LITTLE RED CAR reeked of diesel and squealed when it stopped in front of Astrid's house. Luci had always been very slender, but she looked too skinny that afternoon. When she emerged from her car, she held an aluminum foil-covered tray in hand. Luci looked down at the ground the whole time as if looking for something. She stared at the ground for the duration, moving her lips as if having a conversation in her mind. She did not see Astrid standing by the entrance of her home and gasped when their eyes met.

"*Ay mija,*" she said in Spanish. "I didn't see you there."

She leaned in to give her a warm hug. "*Te acompaño en tu pesar.*"

"Thank you, Luci," said Astrid. "I'm sorry, Luci. I didn't mean to scare you."

"*No, no pasa nada.* My nerves have been acting up."

She touched Astrid's forearm. "Are you alright?"

Her head shook from side to side and her shoulders shrugged. "I don't know," Astrid replied in Spanish. Her accent was different from Luci's.

"I'm sorry," Luci repeated. "God only knows why these things happen. It's like with my Rubi."

"How is she doing? I don't see her at school very often."

"*Pobre mija,*" Luci said. "The dizziness is back. I have her at home resting. Sometimes she has good days and sometimes bad ones. I don't know what to do with her."

"What does the doctor say?"

Luci dismissed her question and raised the plate she carried. "I brought you something."

"You shouldn't have bothered."

"I was going to take it to *La Señora* Regina's for the *novenario*, but I thought I would bring it here instead."

"*Novenario?*" asked Astrid.

Luci looked away. "The nine days of prayer following a death. They are having them for your mother at *La Rosa*."

"Who is?"

"Your *tías*."

"They didn't tell me anything about it."

"I figured they hadn't told you."

"They didn't."

"*Mija*," she said somberly. "I brought it here because I wanted you to have it. I wanted to make sure you were doing OK. I know you have another aunt here, but I was worried about you."

"Thank you. But I don't understand why they didn't tell me. None of them," she pressed. "It's my mom. I want to attend her *novenario*. I SHOULD attend. Why would they not tell me?"

She stepped closer. "I've known you for a long time, *mija*. If I were you," she widened her eyes. "I would stay away from *La Rosa*. I don't want any trouble. I just wanted to tell you. In case you found out about the *novenarios* from anyone. Don't. If I were you, I wouldn't go. Why would you go somewhere they were going to give you *malas caras*?"

"Why Luci? Why would they do that to me?"

"*La Senora* Regina and your aunts and the people there, they were saying some ugly things about you and your other aunt." She shook her head and pleaded. "Don't go. I don't know what you all did to them, but they have a lot of hatred. I've never heard people say such things."

"Why are you telling me this, Luci? You work for Regina. Why are you doing this? Is this coming from you, or did someone send you? Tell me the truth."

Luci took a deep breath and sighed. "You are good people. Sarah was a good person. You don't deserve any of this," she handed the plate to Astrid. "You can do what you want, but it's better if you just avoid them. All of them." She looked at Astrid for a moment. *"Cuidate, mija,"* she leaned in and whispered. "Take care of yourself. They don't wish you well."

Astrid closed her eyes and nodded solemnly. "I know. Thank you, Luci."

"Que la virgencita te acompañe." Astrid could see a tear form in the corner of Luci's eyes.

Astrid glanced back and saw the light on in her mother's altar room. She saw Marianne's shadow through the window, for a moment, Astrid thought it was her mother's. The plate trembled in her hands as tears filled her eyes.

Our Family Can Smell Blood

L OOKING AT HERSELF was never easy, at least not without her heavy shades. Marianne avoided her eyes at all cost. A wave of sadness took over. She stared at her eyes but only one became red, bloodshot and teary. The other was glossy, perfect, unmoved. Shaking her head, she placed her hand over her left eye. "I'm sorry, Sarah."

The thought drifted in simply enough, a terrible scene from her past. The fluorescent lights reflect against the cold tile floor. The loneliness. The resentment. She stared at her hands and realized how much she had aged. But she wasn't old at all. Not even 40. Despite that, her hands revealed her actual age. Her veins were raised and looked like crop fields.

Marianne ran her fingers over the vicarious shelves that lined the back wall. She caught a glimpse of her reflection in a small dusty mirror leaning against a statue of the Virgin Mary. She opened a drawer and found an old pair of her sunglasses. A memory entered her mind's eye.

"You've got mom's hands." Marianne remembered hearing the sweet voice next to her.

She turned to look at Sarah. They were in a hospital room, number 31 on the 3rd Floor of Trinity Hospital.

"Can't stop time," whispered Marianne. She ran her hands across the white, patterned surgical gown.

"Not on hands anyway," Sarah agreed, looking at her own.

Marianne pointed to the pink-colored romance book Sarah carried. "I wish I could escape in books like you."

"Just Turn on the TV. Try to relax. Surgery's not for another three hours."

"How do you expect me to relax, Sarah? They're going to take out a chunk of me."

"Don't exaggerate. It's not a chunk. More like a parcel," she laughed.

"It's not funny. It's not your eye they're removing."

"You're right," agreed Sarah. "I'm sorry. I shouldn't joke. But you shouldn't think this is as bad as it seems."

"How do you want me to handle this then? I can't shoot my brains out. I'm not going to ruin the beauty that God made."

Sarah held back a laugh. "You're so dumb."

"Yeah. Dumb, half-blind and deformed."

"You're not deformed. The doctors already told you no one is even going to know you have it on."

"But I will know. And come on… how are people not going to be able to realize I'm wearing a prosthetic eye."

"They make them very realistic nowadays. We already picked one that matches your eye color exactly."

"But the cleanup. How am I going to keep it clean? I was reading an article that said they form goop and boogers on it. One guy couldn't even pull his eyelid apart. He had to use hot water to melt them off."

"I'm sure he was just a dirty person. I don't think you would let it get that far."

"How am I going to get used to putting a cotton swab inside my own eye."

"Just think of it as a very large ear."

Marianne laughed then started crying. "Stop trying to comfort me, you bitch."

"Stop trying to be defeated."

"I'm not defeated. I'm cursed."

Sarah reached for her sister's hand. "You're not cursed," she said, kissing her palm tenderly. "You're my sister. You are not cursed, and you are not alone in this. You will never be alone."

"I wish mom were here."

"She is, Marianne. She is. She'll make sure the surgery goes right."

Before she let her hands go, she said, "Do me a favor and don't tell Sofia and Julia I'm getting this surgery when you get back home."

"They already know you have an eye issue. They're going to ask me how you are doing."

"Just don't. I don't want them to know I had to have this procedure. I don't want them telling anyone."

"They're going to find out eventually. They're not stupid."

"I just don't want them to make fun of me for it. If I need to see them, I'll wear my sunglasses. They won't be able to tell."

"If you don't want me to tell them I won't. But I don't understand."

"They'll see this as a weakness. You know our family can smell blood a mile away."

She nodded in agreement. The scent of rosewater brought her back to reality.

Back in the altar room, Marianne wiped a tear and spoke to a picture she had in her hand. "You're not alone, either," said Marianne. "And neither is Astrid."

She took a long cleansing breath, then set the mirror down and placed the glasses over her eyes again. She looked throughout the small room. Marianne didn't know what she was searching for, but felt compelled to rummage through the altar. "What am I looking for?" she whispered to herself.

She instinctively picked up a red box, opened it and picked up something wrapped in a white handkerchief. A horrible odor wafted towards Marianne. "Jesus, Sarah," she cringed.

After unwrapping it, she found a small plastic doll tightly bound in rusty barbed wire. Marianne gasped when she turned the doll around and saw something had been carved on the doll's back: **ACF**

"Oh, sister," Marianne shook her head. "What did you do?"

Sulfur, Again

ASTRID WAS ABOUT to go back inside her house when she heard a truck drive up. Her uncle Hector was driving his monster vehicle and hit the brakes aggressively. In an instant, he jumped out of the vehicle and charged at Astrid, with two more men following him.

"Where is she," snorted Hector.

Astrid froze. She had always heard of the Keller bark but had never experienced it first hand. Almost instantly, Marianne appeared on the front porch, her arms placed defiantly over her hips.

"She's here," said Marianne. "I can see you brought your army with you," Marianne remarked snidely.

He smirked. "I don't need anyone to help me tell you what I need to tell you. The family wants you out. They didn't want me to come today, but after the way you attacked Julia, there is no way I'm letting you stay here. Either of you." He faced Astrid.

"This is Astrid 's home now, Hector. Where do you want her to go? *¿Dónde quieres que vaya la niña?*"

He shook his fat finger. "No. Your mother never left it to anyone. It goes to the family. Since you haven't been a part of this family for a very long time, and she humiliated us at the church, you have no right to be here. You can take her back where you came from. Let this family be at peace."

Marianne twisted her face. "I never realized what a backbone you have, Hector," she mocked. "Did you grow a set while I was away? I mean," she raised her hand and pointed at Hector's face and laughed. "Look at the intensity in your eyes. You have such terrifying eyes!"

112

"Take off your sunglasses so I can see *your* eyes." He smirked. "Rumor has it *your* eyes are pretty terrifying, too. Show me that pretty new eye you've got." He taunted.

She stepped forward, "Get out of here before we call the cops."

"George Felton already knows we are here. He agrees with us. They're going to buy this house from Julia as soon as you're gone.

"George Felton isn't the law."

As he nudged at his two fat friends, he chuckled and said, "He used to rule you."

Marianne clenched her jaw and stepped forward. She pointed her finger directly at Hector. "Get back in your truck. You and Julia and the rest of them can fuck off. We're not going anywhere. Don't piss me off, Hector. I can do more than just leave burn marks."

A sneer escaped Hector's lips. "See, that's the shit they're talking about. Why would you do that to your own sister? You people need to just leave. You don't belong here."

Marianne exhaled heavily, dropping her head in irritation. "Look, Hector, we're tired and I know I've been gone a long time. I'm going to let you and your two Minutemen here go. Get out of here! I'll let you retain a little bit of dignity. I'm not as sweet as I used to be."

"Sweet? Sweet like battery acid," he nudged at the men again.

Marianne's nostrils flared. "Get lost, fat ass."

Hector reached into his pocket to reveal a small handgun. "Or what?" his nose shot into the air. "Just what are you going to do?"

Astrid's eyes widened as she flinched back. Her fingers dug into Marianne's shoulders, nudging her back.

"That's right," said Hector. "Think your little magic-*brujeria*-nonsense is going to work on me?" He shook the weapon. "Come on!" he growled. "Go on and try to burn me like you did to my Julia. Come on. Where is it? Where's your fire?" He waved his weapon. "Look at this, baby. Cold, hard steel. Your *brujeria* ain't gonna stop a bullet from sliding inside your pretty little skull?" They all cackled. "No crime to shoot an intruder, you know.That's just what you are, a God damned intruder."

"Astrid's not an intruder. She was born and raised here."

"But you are," he pointed the weapon straight at Marianne's head and cocked his gun.

That's when Astrid slipped behind Marianne. She could smell sulfur again. She feared the odor more than the sound of her Uncle Hector's gun. This time, the smell made her almost gag. Marianne extended her hand at Astrid. She clasped it in support. The men stopped laughing when they saw Marianne raise her left hand. Their looks were filled with horror.

The sulfur intensified. Hector's mouth jerked strangely. It twisted to the side, his jaw trembled wildly. He screamed maniacal and horrible sounds, then gurgled as he tried to force it back into place. Then came the crashing. Their heavy bodies fell to their knees with loud thumps, as if something had removed their cartilage, leaving the bone to smash against hollow skin. Their faces stretched, morphed, and they used their tense fingers to claw and scratch away at their eyes. Sweat dripped from their foreheads as they jerked wildly on the floor, gasping for breath. The men scratched at their throats as if they had an invisible choke on them. Their eyes glowed red as the veins on their head and neck swelled.

Marianne leaned in, "I don't want to see you fat fucks in my house again." Almost instantly, the men were able to breathe again. Hector struggled to raise his fat body off the floor, but wasted no time in galloping away. His two friends scampered behind him and sped away in their pickup truck.

Marianne reached for Astrid's hand, and she quickly accepted it. A part of Astrid was afraid her aunt would attack her as well.

Unseen Gifts

THEY SAT AT THE kitchen table in silence. Neither Astrid nor Marianne knew how to start any type of conversation. They were, after all, strangers. Blood bound them, but absolutely no history linked the pair. Astrid felt like crying. As she sat across from her estranged aunt and sole ally, she felt her grip on hope slipping.

Marianne sat upright in her chair. *How can she be so calm,* thought Astrid. *Doesn't she realize what's going to happen? Tio Hector is going to call the police. The Pinched Sisters are going to make them come back. They are going to do something to us. I know them. They are not just going to go cower. What is she thinking?*

But Marianne's mind wasn't calm at all. She was thinking about how to approach the conversation that needed to happen. She wanted Astrid to know that she loved her mother very much and thought of her as a twin. A better twin. What Astrid had witnessed in the cemetery had been brewing for years. Decades, really. Astrid was unaware of the troubled history Marianne had with her family. Astrid knew they kept their distance, but the devil's in the details, as they say. So Marianne did what she did best. She reached for her purse, lit a cigarette and started smoking.

Astrid wanted to tell her something about the smell. Her mother would have raised a storm if someone, let alone a stranger, had the gall to smoke in her small, pristine kitchen. The girl stayed silent as she observed her aunt's cigarette slowly roll toward her lips. It was almost rhythmic. She was fluid. The way she controlled the swirl around her was hypnotic. Astrid suspected it was more of her magic.

Astrid tried not to think about the three men on her porch. What was going

115

to happen when they told someone? Why was Marianne so blatant about her gifts? Grandma used to say that you needed to keep quiet about your gifts. Never brag. Never exploit them. They can be used against you, after all. Marianne threw that playbook out the window; caution was burning in the wind. Astrid couldn't understand the brazen attitude her aunt had toward her magic. But then again, what was her power? Who had the power to make people twist their bodies and then make their body parts twist and crash on the ground? What do you even call that? To cause burns with a simple touch? This was nothing compared to her mother's card-reading abilities or her grandmother's healing gifts. This was power. Real power. A power Astrid wanted to know more, wanted to unravel.

"Marianne," she began, "What did you do to them?"

"I gave them what they deserved," she said, reaching for a glass of water and taking a sip. She chuckled into the glass. "I kind of enjoyed seeing Hector's stupid face look so scared. A bunch of cowards is what they are. Who does that? Who comes to someone's house and tries to evict them?"

"He's never liked us."

"Well, the feeling is mutual, kid. Don't know what Sofia sees in him. But then again, she's a sad, angry woman. Mediocrity and self-hatred go hand in hand."

"What's going to happen if they tell people what you did? Do you really think anyone really can kick us out of here? Where will you go? Where will I go?"

"Did you see them running?" she beamed. "There's no way they'll be back here any time soon. They played with fire." Astrid wanted to ask her to take off her glasses but was scared of what she might see. "They got burned. If they show their faces here again, guess what's going to happen to them? Come on. Take a wild one."

"They want this house. I heard them say they want this house."

"It doesn't matter what they said. But they'll stay away. For a few days, anyway."

Astrid hesitated, her fingers fumbled on the table. "Marianne?"

"Yeah, kid?"

116

"What exactly do you have?"

"What do you mean?"

"You dropped them. You made all those men fall to the floor. You just looked at them. What—What is that? How do you do that? I've never seen anything like it."

Marianne giggled. "You don't know anything about anything. It's kind of cute. Have you ever seen the old movie The Wizard of Oz? The one with Judy Garland."

"I have."

"You remind me of the pink witch. Glinda or Glenda. I don't remember her name, but I saw her in a huge bubble and I thought how elegant and beautiful she was. Kind of like you and the way your mom raised you. Just a pretty little *bruja* living in a pretty pink bubble."

Astrid chuckled. "Are you insane? Mom never even wanted to read my cards, let alone teach me to do anything *brujeria*-ish. If you'd been around you'd know that I wasn't raised to be a witch. I'm not a *bruja* like you."

"Don't you laugh at me." Marianne abruptly lifted her hand to the sky. All the cabinets flew open in the small Cortez kitchen. Dishes flew out and slammed to the ground.

"Show me how you did that!" Astrid took a step back.

Marianne whirled her arm as the drawers flew off the rail and crashed into the walls.

"How are you doing that?"

Her aunt swung the other hand and the picture frames fell from their positions on the walls in the living room. The 8 x 10 photograph of her grandma Carmen cracked in half.

"Tell me!" Astrid's shriek was shaky.

Marianne clapped her hands, sending Astrid flying back. She was pinned against the kitchen wall, her body floating for several moments before dropping with a thud. Astrid groaned, immobilized. A loud buzz filled her ears as she struggled to her feet. "Why did you do that?" All color had drained from her face. "I thought you protected the ones you love?"

"What are you going to do about it?" Marianne taunted.

"I can't hurl objects at you! I don't possess that gift."

Marianne mocked, "Oh, brother… what can you do?"

"I don't know!" cringed Astrid. "Don't you understand? I don't know how to do anything!"

"You do, kid." Marianne crouched down in front of Astrid, her eyes fixed on her niece. "Your grandmother told you a long time ago. She told you all about your gift. You've been using them this whole time. Don't lie to me!"

"She never told me anything. I don't know anything. I don't have any gifts!"

Marianne flung her arms high and raised Astrid's body. She was floating again. "You stupid kid. Do you know what I'd do if I could ride the wind!" Marianne threw down her arms, and Astrid's body pounded the floor.

Astrid was crying now, sobbing quietly on the ground. "I can't," she said weakly. "Please stop. I can't fight you. I don't know what you want me to say. I don't have any powers. I'm not like you."

Marianne turned her back and stepped in front of the kitchen window. She began believing her niece. She stared at the ground. Pacing slowly, she looked at Astrid with an empathetic frown. "My God," she sighed. "Sarah really didn't teach you anything." Marianne tilted her head. "You really are in a bubble."

Astrid was still lying on the floor. She sat up and wrapped her arms around her feet. "I told you, mom didn't teach me anything." Marianne narrowed her eyes, trying not to speak while listening to her niece. "She didn't want me to know anything. I'm not lying to you. I don't know anything! I don't have any power. I don't have what you have. I'm not strong like you. I'm just me, just plain old boring and nothing Astrid."

Marianne shook her head. She stared into the road and followed as two police vehicles drove away from the city. She twisted her mouth and bit the corners of her lip. Perhaps this was all too much for the girl. This was something completely unexpected. Marianne assumed Astrid knew her roots, her lineage. She had no idea that Astrid was so out of the loop. Void of reality. Marianne felt terribly sorry for her niece for a moment. It was horrible, like being blessed with a beautiful face but no eyes to see it with. How could she not know how blessed she was? Why would they hide it from her? Why would they hide such a gift? It was unjust. This poor dumb kid had no idea what the hell was going on, or what was looking for her.

"You can ride the wind," Marianne said suddenly.

Astrid perked her head up.

"I know you've done it before," continued Marianne. "You think you're dreaming, but that's because no one told you any better. You are not bound to your skin. You have a beautiful gift."

"I've heard that before. Grandma told me those words. I remember. I remember her saying that."

"Some of us can read tarot cards. Your mother was very good at that. Some of us can wipe away energy and heal the sick. We know the herbs and we can cure people. My mom was a wonderful *curandera*. But you, you are not bound to your skin. You can leave your body. You can. You can ride the wind, travel and go to places none of us have ever dreamed of. You can even enter other bodies. It's dangerous, but you can. I've seen you. I know this to be true."

Astrid stared up at Marianne in disbelief. "I don't understand. I've never done that before. I never— I've never done anything like that."

Marianne widened her eyes after releasing a shallow sigh. "I remember when my mom died. Sarah always said momma was close to you, she felt like you were her own. But I was never around, you know this. I never knew the bond you two had. I remember talking to Sarah outside the funeral parlor when we started looking for you after everyone left. We thought maybe you were playing outside with one of your cousins, but no, not at all. We found you with my mom, but you were doing something that shook both Sarah and me to our core."

"What was I doing?"

Marianne fought back tears. "We saw you standing over the coffin, but mom was not lying down. Her body was upright. Her arms were around you. We stood there frozen stiff. I don't even think I even took a breath for over a minute, and believe me, I am not one easily shocked. That's when Sarah said, 'Astrid. No. Don't you do that. Don't do that to grandma.' When you turned back to us, we saw her body slowly fall back into the coffin, lifeless again.

119

Sarah ran to you. You were so cold and your lips were purple. 'I wanted her to hug me again. Just once more,' you whispered. Sarah confirmed you had the gift. You could manipulate the dead. Make the inanimate animate. It's a terrible gift, a frightening one. I can see why Sarah never led you down that path."

"That's a gift?" Astrid wiped her tears and stood up.

Marianne raised her eyebrows. "Are you kidding me? Imagine the possibilities! I've been in situations where I wanted nothing more than to crawl out of my skin. Tear off my meat and bones and let it all fall to the ground. Escape. I've had moments where I'd give my life to fly right out of this very planet. And you have that gift. You *can* leave your body. You can fly above the world... ride the wind, as momma would say." She stared deeply into Astrid's eyes. "Somewhere deep inside, you know this is true. Has anything happened recently? Has anything strange occurred? Any dreams or visions?" asked Marianne.

"I've never even recognized it as a gift. I start feeling tingly all over. I keep trying to remain calm, but a few days ago something happened and I fainted. I mean, I *think* I fainted. I could see my body on the ground. Everything was so crisp and all the colors were alive. Like a film negative. It happened in the Felton fields."

"What did you feel?" Marianne probed. She helped Astrid to her feet and led her to the kitchen table. "Tell me everything, Astrid. I need to know."

"I was playing a game."

"You're too old for games, Astrid. You're almost eighteen."

"Not that kind of game. It was more of a plan. I was trying to make a boy fall in love with me. Or like me, at least. It was in the sugarcane field."

"You don't need games for that. Don't tell me Sarah never taught you how to catch a man? It's the easiest thing in the world!"

"No," said Astrid. "Are you kidding me?" She shook her head vigorously. "Dylan was the guy who thought he was saving me from a fire. I asked my best friend to help me convince him I was in trouble so he could feel like a hero." She shrugged. "I thought it would work."

"Did it?"

"No. Well, I wouldn't know, would I? I haven't seen him since that day. Then mom—well, she's gone, so I haven't been to school."

Marianne squeezed Astrid's hand tightly. "So while you were playing this little game of yours, you were able to leave your body?"

"I don't know. I've never felt anything like it before. I was flying, floating, yes. I remember I saw Benny running towards me and I saw Dylan, too. I was lying in the sugarcane fields. I saw something in between the stalks. Something with cold, red eyes staring up at me."

"What did it look like?"

"It was a blue snake?"

"A blue snake?"

Astrid nodded, shaking. "Long. With a blue rattle."

Marianne's brows closed in.

"Then the thunder came and brought me back."

Her eyes were closed as she turned away from Astrid. "Your mother wouldn't have wanted me to tell you, but I don't think we have a choice now. We have to prepare."

"Prepare for what?"

Marianne turned to Astrid and took a deep breath. "I don't think your mother died of cancer. Not the way the doctors think, anyway. Cancer usually forms in the body, but hers didn't."

"What do you mean?"

"I've smelled cancer before. I know the scent. When I saw your mother I could feel the magic. I could smell the curse. Her cancer did not originate inside her, it was placed there. It was a poison."

Astrid leaned in closer. She didn't want a response, but she asked just the same: "What are you telling me, Marianne?"

"It never should have happened. I think she was killed, Astrid." Marianne confirmed. "Will you help me? Will you help me with what needs to be done?"

Astrid's heart awoke, frantically drumming inside her. "What are we gonna do?" her voice quivered.

Marianne touched Astrid's shoulder. "Don't be afraid," she whispered, "Don't be scared of what's to come."

"What are we going to do!?" Astrid repeated louder.

Marianne forced a weak smile. "We must do as witches do." Marianne looked away somberly.

"I never understood what it meant to be a witch," said Astrid.

"Neither did I until I felt the power rushing in me."

"I don't feel any power. It's not like I can control it."

"You can control it, and you've got to. Otherwise, it controls you."

"How can I do that?"

"It takes will. That's all. You send the signal. You focus on the message, and you will bring it into existence. The magic is there. It needs to hear your call."

"My mother didn't have this gift, did she?"

"Your mother was a good woman with a good heart, but she did not have the power you do. Oh no. God has blessed you eternally."

She stared into her aunt's eyes incredulously.

"Someone wanted your mother dead, Astrid. They succeeded. But you, you gifted girl, you can walk behind the night. You can ride the wind. You can find truth in the darkness."

"If this is true, you've got to teach me. Please. What do we need to do? I don't know how to do what you say I can do."

"The body can help us forget our pain, but the soul is something quite different. Your mind may be blind to these things, but your soul is wide awake. I can see that as clear as day."

"I can't. You say I can, but I can't! I don't know how to use these gifts you say I have."

She reached for Astrid. "I can show you, kid. It's time to ride the wind." Marianne spoke in a low voice, "I've always wanted to know what it was like to ride the wind. Most people call it Astral Projection, the ability to leave your body and fly anywhere you want. See anything and anyone whenever you want. I thought it was the coolest thing, man. There are so many times I just want to fucking fly right out of here, you know. When someone was screaming at me, whenever I was nervous about having to do something, whenever I was scared shitless and just wanted to scream, run, die, fall, hide. I wished I had this gift. I wanted to ride the wind. I would have given anything for it."

"I've never thought of it that way."

"What problems could you have to run away from?" said Marianne.

"I'm a teenage girl in America, my whole life is a flight risk."

"What problems could you possibly have?"

"I don't have a mom. That's a problem."

"Shit. That's very true." Marianne smoked her cigarette and continued, "That one's a doozy. A big one, no doubt. But you've never seen pain, kid. Not really. You've never had a knife pulled on you, or had someone's boots pressing down on your face so hard you can taste the dirt they've walked on. Or seen your own family turn on you so fast you didn't know you could ever catch your breath again from all the crying. I've seen pain, kid. Authentic pain that cuts the skin and cuts the soul."

Astrid muttered, "Damn."

"Damn right, damn. So yeah, the thought of having the ability to fly my ass out of my body and into the ether sounds like a pretty sweet deal to me."

Astrid was too stunned to muster a reply. Marianne spoke again, "You're lucky, Astrid. God has blessed you eternally."

"That's what Grandma Carmen used to tell me. I never understood her."

"Crazy old woman" Marianne remarked, "She never did make it easy on any of us. She could have taught you. Poor Sarah tried to keep your gifts at bay with baby-witch magic, plastic dolls, and barbed wire. Basic spells, you know. She was never very gifted. I don't know why momma didn't guide you. I guess she – Well, to be honest, I don't know why she didn't. I'd be pissed at her, but it's not good to hate the dead."

"I was very young. Maybe she didn't think I was ready."

"No one ever is, Astrid. But now we've got some bad witches on our back and no time to prepare."

"But we can start. We can start now, Marianne. I can practice and I can try to figure this out. We can try. We have to try. Please. What do we have to do?"

Marianne widened her eyes. "It starts with a Midnight Coronation."

A Passive Altar

ASTRID TOUCHED ONE OF the empty chairs as they entered her mother's altar room. She could almost hear the gentle hum of old prayers that would fill the small space. The candles used to be rotated regularly, but the statues of St. Michael, the Holy Infant of Atocha and El Niño Fidencio, a Mexican folk saint, were never moved. Astrid's grandmother, Carmen, held them in the highest regard and trusted them with helping her in her healing journey. It was a fusion of Catholic iconography and Mexican magic. It was Sarah's sacred place, but it had become somewhat of a passive altar. Sarah was not as meticulous about cleaning and cultivating the space. In many ways, the room remained an untouched relic of days before her grandmother's death.

The room wasn't large, only one hundred or so square feet, but when you stepped inside, it carried the weight and vibrations of something much more magnificent, something holy. Astrid felt the energy almost instantly and, for a moment, was taken aback. She hadn't realized the power the room possessed. How could she have been so blind to the divinity of her heritage?

The dimly lit room smelled of rosewater and incense. Astrid stepped in front of the tall statue of St. Jude. She discovered an old photograph of herself tightly wrapped to the statue's heart. A bittersweet smile appeared on her face.

Marianne carried something in her hands as she stepped in front of the altar. She looked like she was praying, but Astrid suddenly heard the soft sobs coming from her cold aunt. It shook her.

Instinctively, Astrid reached for her aunt. She placed her hand over

124

Marianne's shoulder but immediately felt her flinch and step away. "I hadn't been here in so long," she said. "I'm sorry."

"Don't be sorry. I never come into this room and I live here."

Marianne took the object from her hand and placed it on the altar next to a small, weathered statue of the Virgin of Guadalupe. Astrid could now see it was the photograph of her grandmother that had fallen earlier.

"She needs to be here now," said Marianne.

"We need to print a photo of mom and bring it, too."

Marianne was still wearing her sunglasses and wiped the tears. "Turn away," she said to Astrid, who reluctantly obeyed.

Marianne lifted her sunglasses quickly and wiped her eyes dry.

"You can look," she said after placing her sunglasses back over her eyes.

"Why don't you want me to see your eyes," said Astrid.

Marianne quickly snapped. "Why don't you worry about more important things."

"What are you hiding," she persisted.

"Power comes at a price," said Marianne. "It's not always pretty." She lifted her sunglasses to reveal her unhappy truth.

Astrid stepped back, "What happened to you?"

"I paid," she said frankly. "I'm still paying."

"Does it hurt?"

"No. It's just unsightly. I went away to try and fix it. This didn't happen overnight, you know. I've had this curse on me for as long as you've been alive. I started losing my eyesight around the time you were born. A blackness started to take over. I went to several doctors and they told me the disease would spread if I did not remove it. Malignancies," she sighed, "need to be cut out." Marianne half smiled and put her glasses back on. "It could have been worse. Much, much worse."

Astrid didn't know what to say. She would probably walk around wearing sunglasses all day if she were in Marianne's predicament. The thought came out of her mouth before being filtered. "Was it worth it," asked Astrid.

Marianne immediately answered, "Oh, yes. It was. But we're not going to spend any time feeling sorry for me, Kid. Right now you and I have some work to do. We're going to clean up this altar. We're going to move energies, let in some sunlight and we're going to bring back our forgotten magic. There's power in these walls. It's hidden under dust and neglect."

"Cleaning the altar will help us?" Astrid asked.

"Every good witch needs to have an altar. It's how we claim our power. It's a place to hone our craft. It's your link between divinity and nature. You are a combination of both. Your altar is a reflection of who you are. Not enough people have altars nowadays. Can you imagine how good this world would be if more people had altars? A place to respect their divinity. The God in us. A place to worship and respect the necessary unseen. This is our holy seed."

Astrid found a photo of her mother and her aunts as she cleaned. "Look how young my mom looks."

"You'd think we were actually a family."

"You look so young," said Astrid. "Look at my mom. She looks like a teenager."

"Just look at that lie. A loving family," Marianne scoffed. "I don't romanticize the idea of family. It's a necessity, nothing more."

"Bleak."

"It's reality. You think our family is something to be celebrated. Look at us, broken and fighting, hating and cursing. You think we loved each other at one point?"

"Did you?"

"Can't say we did."

"Why?"

"Love is a luxury. We weren't exactly Rockefeller's. We survived because momma worked hard and God was on our side. I can't remember a time I actually cared about my sisters. They were out of the house before I was even a teenager. And then I saw that ridiculous Sophia throw herself on the coffin when mom was being buried. Where was that devotion when mom couldn't get out of bed? When she couldn't wash herself anymore? My sisters said they loved her so much and they cried so hard, but they can't love. They idealize it but don't see that real love, true love, is loving someone unconditionally as you watch them fade away. Many people don't see it. Love is quiet. It's

126

listening to people when they cough and hearing thick phlegm loosen and feeling relieved when it goes down their windpipe. Love is listening to stories even though you know you've heard it countless times before. It's staying up with them. It's rubbing their back. It's washing their feet and making sure their hair doesn't smell."

"My mom did all those things for grandma."

"I know she did. She loved her very much."

"But you," Astrid hesitated. "You were gone. You didn't do any of those things."

"No," she sighed. "I did not."

"Are you saying you didn't love her? You didn't love Grandma Carmen?"

"No. I'm not saying I didn't love my mom. In my case, all I can say is that I *couldn't* love her. That's a very different thing. Sometimes it's hard to love your momma. You, more than anyone, should understand that."

"What's that supposed to mean?"

Marianne reached for the box where her mother kept her tarot cards.

"Those were my mom's," said Astrid. "She didn't like me touching them. She doesn't like for anyone to touch them."

"I can imagine she wouldn't want anyone touching *this* box... especially you," replied Marianne. "But this is the cause of all your confusion. You're not going to like what I have to tell you, but I'm going to tell you anyway. There's something in here that keeps your eyes shut."

"The cards?"

"No. What's laying with the cards," Marianne said as she opened up the box. A fowl stench quickly permeated the room and Astrid fixed her eyes on the old doll wrapped in barbed wire.

"What's that?"

"That's you, Kid."

"Me?"

"Well, that *was* you. The spell is dying. It starting to rot."

"I don't understand."

"It's a binding spell. It's what kept you from manifesting your gifts. It's supposed to keep your third eye closed."

127

"I don't have a third eye."

"Oh," she laughed, "You have a third eye and boy was it ready to open wide."

"Why would mom do that? Why would she bind me?"

"For love, kid. Mothers do crazy things to prove their love. She thought she was keeping you safe."

Astrid crossed her arms, "I'm not safe. Look at me. I'm lost now. I don't know what I'm doing. I don't know who I am."

A sympathetic smile spread across Marianne's face. "As I said, sometimes it's hard to love our mothers. It's even harder to understand them. You are Astrid. You're Sarah's daughter. You're my niece. You're Carmen's granddaughter and the descendant of people with infinite sight. It doesn't matter that you were blind. It doesn't matter that you were bound. You're free now, and I can help you ride the wind."

The Midnight Coronation

MARIANNE LIT A candle and both aunt and niece watched it grow. "What's it doing?" Astrid asked, stepping closer to the fire. "Some people go looking for the light, but sometimes the light looks for us," Marianne replied. The flame grew, becoming thinner and brighter until a snake-like figure formed. Astrid's heart pounded and her palms turned sweaty as the flame began trembling and bent in her direction.

"What's it doing?"

Marianne smiled. "She's saying hello."

Astrid knew it was time to search her soul; it was something she could no longer avoid. What teenage girl enjoys looking inward? The soul cannot be painted or polished. The deep within cannot be improved by watching YouTube tutorials. To look inside and manifest one's power requires stillness, determination and ultimately, resignation.

Astrid's fingers nervously tapped on the table her mother used to read tarot cards. She felt raw like the table—distressed and exposed. For a moment, she thought she saw a face form through the table's curved wood grain lines, but this image disappeared as quickly as it appeared.

"I am never alone," Marianne broke the silence. "It's something I've grown accustomed to. I hear things. They tell me things."

"Who?" asked Astrid.

"Those who walk among us," her voice was solemn.

"The dead?"

"I've never liked that word. No one ever dies; they move on to another state of being. They leave their bodies, and they migrate. We are all migrants in that way. From one land to the next, in constant search for something new, something better. Eventually, we all migrate. But not all of them make it, you see. Those who stay are always looking for a way back in."

"And you can talk to them?"

She nodded. "I can speak *for* them. I can even bring them down. Spirits of the dead can live in me."

"You mean you can—"

"They speak *through* me. Feel through me. Live through me," said Marianne. "I am a host. Nothing more."

"Can you bring anyone down?"

She shook her head. "Only if they are still here and only if they allow it. My gift is very different from yours. I can bring spirits down, but you can do something even far more spectacular. Your gift is marvelous, but also dangerous."

"Why?"

"Because when you are out of your body, you are very vulnerable. Astral Projection is very dangerous. It's something heavy, something dangerous. Leaving your body comes at a price. God doesn't give this gift to just anyone. It is a powerful thing to detach. You must be aware of your surroundings at all times. I remember mom was afraid of you. I remember she had you on this very altar and she prayed very hard for you. I know she wanted to guide you. But magic is not something you can teach; it is something that develops on its own. Too many people flood their gardens thinking that water will make their flowers bloom."

Astrid looked toward the altar and noticed a small photo of herself. She imagined her small-framed grandmother gazing at the frame and praying over it. It was a comforting thought.

Marianne sat up and picked up a small bottle from one of the shelves. Astrid instantly recognized it was her grandmother's rose oil. "Magic is spiritual intentions," said Marianne. "Let's introduce you to the world with our very own Midnight Coronation." Marianne rubbed the oil on the crook of her arm and her temples, then breathed the fragrance in.

"Why is it called that?"

Marianne laughed. "Your mother and I used to joke that we never had quinceaneras. This was the next best thing. This was our way of telling the world we were ready for our gifts. We accepted them. It's silly, but it's ours. It's what we shared and what I will share with you. I remember we stood right where you are. Sarah and I were younger and tried to ride the wind, to Astral Project. We were sure we had these powers but they were dormant. We would try to leave our bodies at night during full moons. We were so silly. Nothing ever happened. But once, when I tried to astral project, I felt a whirl of energy around my head. Even though I didn't leave my body, I felt as if I was wearing a crown of stars and energy. This gift is like receiving a cosmic crown of midnight stars and gives you the power to slip in and out of your shell. That's why we ended up calling it a Midnight Coronation." A gust of wind suddenly picked up and ruffled tree leaves outside the small room. "They're waiting," Marianne said.

Marianne guided Astrid away from the altar room and onto a grassy area outside, where she instructed her to lay down. "Become like the stars," she said. With a wooden box in hand, Marianne knelt next to her niece and retrieved a bundle of aromatic herbs including lavender, basil, and laurel. As she softly whispered Spanish prayers, Marianne gently applied the herbs all over Astrid's body. From her head to her toes, Marianne massaged rose oil onto Astrid's skin, carefully dabbing it behind her ears, on her temples, in the crooks of her arms and knees, and on the soles of her feet. "A spirit dwells in you," she said, "but God and the wisdom of the universe has seen fit to let you wander outside your body. This is a gift and a privilege. This ceremony is how we let the universe know we're ready. Like a king or a queen, you must bear the weight of this crown—the heaviness of knowledge, Astrid. The loneliness of sight."

Marianne pulled a safety pin and a small lighter from her pocket. She lit the tip on fire.

"Take this," she gave the warm safety pin to Astrid, then reached for an unlit white candle. "Before we begin, you need to break your shell. Give room for the spirit to leave through."

"Blood," she signaled to the safety pin in Astrid's hands. "A little blood is needed for this task."

"You want my blood?"

Marianne nodded. "Just a drop."

Astrid reluctantly inched the needle close to her finger. She felt a fear of the pain but felt even more terror when she saw her aunt's eyes grow wide and a horrible grin stretched across her face.

Astrid pricked her finger then Marianne instructed her to rub a thick drop of blood around the top of the candle.

Marianne then took the unlit candle and rubbed it around Astrid'd body. "Protect the girl," she whispered in Spanish. "Shield the girl."

Marianne set the candle back on the altar then stood next to Astrid. Sweat beads had formed over her temples, the ceremony had winded her. "Take this match now," she grabbed a matchbox from her pockets. "You need to light the wick. It will tell God you accept his gift. You must tell God you are ready for this. You must light the candle. Thank him for this *don*."

Astrid suddenly realized pricking her finger was easier to do than lighting a candle. Was she ready to accept this gift? What was she going to be required to do now that she acknowledged her don, her divine gift? What if she didn't want the gift after all? Would she be able to stop it? Would she want this gift in the future? She held the unlit match in her fingers and stared into her aunt's eyes. "What happens if we stop," she said.

"Then," stated Marianne , "I have failed."

Astrid looked at the match, a part of her wanted to do it. To finally accept her path, but another was frightened. If her mother hadn't wanted her to take part in this ceremony, then why was she even here? She must have been protecting her. She must have been warning her.

Then Astrid saw a strange ripple, a dark movement from the corner of her eyes. "Light the candle." She heard a voice calling. It was so calm, so full of life. Comforting and enchanting all at once. It was the voice she longed to hear: her mother's. "Light the candle."

Astrid's eyes welled with tears.

With a quick flick, she lit the match and carried the flame to the white candle.

"Everyone can leave their body," explained Marianne. Astrid lay down on the ground and rested her head on a small pillow. Marianne surrounded her body with small, votive candles. Incense was lit, and the smoke swirled around her. "Most people leave their body while they sleep. They call it dreaming, but it's really soul traveling. It's usually benign. They dip their toes, feel the sensations, then immediately return to their bodies. But people like you are different. People like you can swim in that state. They can stay longer. Travel further."

"Where can I go?"

"Anywhere, kid."

"Imagine being a world away from your loved ones and then being instantly transported next to them. Distance has no power in that Astral world. Imagine the power you can harness. You can see what others want kept secret. You can bear witness to events miles away or read behind someone's shoulder while they write. Imagine. What a gift. What a treat."

"Why did mom never tell me about this?"

"Fear. Jealousy. Take your pick," said Marianne. "She bound you. She bound you good and tight. But something broke the spell."

"What did? What do you think broke the spell?"

"Those snakes you mentioned earlier. I've heard of them before, and now everything makes sense to me."

"What are they?"

"They are Malinal Snakes—magic hunters. Our mother was sent a Malinal when she was younger, but she caught it before it could bite her. She said other witches had sent the Malinal. They smell the air for magic with their tongues. They rattle their tail and it picks up the vibrations that witches generate."

"They found me. They found us."

"I think they found your mother first. I think that's really what killed her."

Astrid shook her head. "I knew she didn't have cancer. When she was on the floor, I remember she was grabbing at her ankle. She—- she was pointing at the window. It must have. It must have attacked her."

"Malinal Snakes don't leave a mark. They have been bred to kill without a trace."

"Who? Who would make such a thing?"

"The Witches of Cascabel," said Marianne.

"I've never heard of them."

"And yet you have their assassins in your backyard. What we need to do is find out who sent them here. Someone has to pay for your mother's death. We've got work to do." Marianne took a deep breath and placed her hands on Astrid's forehead. Astrid instinctively closed her eyes. "Astrid," Marianne chuckled and half smiled. "Astrid the Astral Projector. Out of all the names your mother could have given you, she chose Astrid. And she didn't even bother telling you the truth." Marianne shook her head. "Your mother was something else."

"She should have shown me all of this. I feel like I'm being thrown into a lake without swimming lessons. Does it hurt? Is it like dreaming? Will I remember anything? How long can I stay outside?" asked Astrid.

"I don't know all the answers, but you shouldn't be outside your body for too long. Not now. Not at this stage. There's a reason a house starts to fall apart when a family isn't living inside it after some time passes. I imagine that's what happens here as well."

"I shouldn't leave my house for too long, huh?"

"No, you need to return, and the sooner the better. First, find a place where you feel safe. You must learn to guide yourself. All it takes is intent. Simply let yourself go. But for tonight, I will guide you. Take deep breaths and strive to clear your mind. Your mind and spirit will become one. Visualize your destination. This is your gift. Soar among the stars, Astrid. Close your eyes. In this realm, there is no time and no distance. Become the wind."

"Breathe, Astrid."

DARKNESS IN THE MIND'S EYE.

"It's easy, Kid. It's very, very easy. It's as easy as letting go of a breath. Exhale, Astrid. Exhale."

DARKNESS IN THE MIND'S EYE.

"Ex-Ex Ex hale hale hale. We will see what you are made of. We will see what God has placed in you."

Why me? Why me?

COLORFUL SWIRLS BEGIN TO APPEAR IN THE DISTANCE.

It's easy. It's very, very easy.

A STRANGE, NEBULA-LIKE MIST APPROACHES.

I.
  I see.

A CUT. A CUT THROUGH A FLUID, BLACK VEIL.

I feel myself cracking–breaking. I feel my body begin to get very chilly. A coldness is taking over me. I hear the rumble. I taste the salt of my body. I face the edge of the world and know I am guided.

I am here for you.

I feel a heaviness on my chest. Is this normal?
  I see myself now—I am drifting.
  I feel as though I'm walking behind the night. Hidden in the stars. Flying in the

135

wing.

I see the altar. I am flying now. I see the candles. But they are not the right color. They are not light, white and orange. They are black. The flames are black. But they still give off a radiant light.

I see Marianne. I see her next to me. I am on the chair.
  I am laying on the grass.
  That's me. That's Astrid. Can I be me Here and There?
  Am I Astrid in this world?
  Am I Astrid in any world?

I float higher now. Higher and higher. I am riding the wind! I see the trees above our house. Then there are the Felton Fields. I am afraid of seeing the blue snake. I hate those Malinal Snakes. I don't want to see the eyes. I don't want to travel too far. But I want to see more.

I need to see my mother.
  I need to be with her again.
  To the Cemetery.
  Yes! To the Cemetery. That place is safe. That place is familiar. That place has her.
  That is where I'll go.

The Little Ones Are the Worst

I FEEL LIKE STATIC. *Like pulsing. A contradiction of movement and rest. Alive and dead. An incongruity. A blessing and a curse.*

I've never been this free.

I can see Marianne. She's praying over me. I can see tiny bolts of energy spark as she touches my hands. In this world, I can see magic. I can see when energy moves.

I float above the sleepy town of Diller, back towards the cemetery. I am transported past the Felton fields, thrust towards the cemetery. I know it's the safest place to be, in this altered, new state. I want to be in a place where I can be safe. The sun had set hours ago, but there are still two cars outside the gates of the Diller Catholic Cemetery.

There is no wind to stir the chimes that hang in the cemetery trees. It is deathly still. As I descend towards the ground, I can see movement and a faint light within the graves until I see two figures walking straight towards my mother's grave.

As I fly down further and closer I realize it's my two aunts, Sofia and Julia. It is those damned Pinched Sisters. Julia's tall frame and Sofia's stocky build are unmistakable even in the darkness. What in the world are they doing here?

"Hurry up!" snapped Julia. "And point the flash down low, I don't want the Border Patrol to know we are here."

"I wasn't going to let you come alone. Slow down!"

"I would have preferred it. Keep your voice down. This won't take long. I want to see if it's true."

"I don't think it is Julia. You know how Estella lies."

"She's not the only one who saw it," snapped Julia. "Josefina told me during the novenario. *Her husband was the one who killed it. It's probably* brujeria *from*

Marianne."

"Then we probably shouldn't be touching it."

"We're not going to touch it, Sofia. I just need to see if it's true. I need to see it for myself. I want to know if it's really what they say it is."

Once near Sarah's grave, Sofia takes out a phone from her pockets and hands it to Julia. "Here. Take a picture for me if you see it. I don't want to get near it."

"I'm not taking a picture of it! Are you insane? My husband doesn't know I'm here and I don't want him finding out."

"Be careful. Watch your feet," urged Sofia. "There may be more. Maybe it was the mother. The chiquitos are even worse."

The two look through the gravesite, meticulously using their phones as flashlights over every inch of the area. "Do you know where Josephine's husband left it?"

"I'm not sure," said Julia. "She just said he saw it coiled over Sarah's grave. The snake wasn't even scared. It was like it was protecting the grave." She immediately made the sign of the cross.

"Don't say things like that," said Sofia. "We are doing the novenarios. Her soul is safe. She's fine. She's resting in peace now. Marianne can't use her anymore. She's in the Lord's hands."

They continue walking around the grave site until Sofia let out a horrifying scream. Julia rushed to her side as her sister points to a weathered oil drum being used as a trash can. "You were right! I can't. I just can't believe it!" Sofia shun the light into the drum. Julia peeked her head. Inside the dirty bin was the dead body of a strange, blue rattlesnake. A Malinal Snake.

"Dios Santo," said Julia. "It's like the one that almost attacked mom. Don't you remember? When we were still living in the old house. Remember?"

Sofia shook her head in disgust. "I'm so glad Regina met those people when she did."

"What people," asked Julia. "What are you talking about?"

Sofia lowered her voice: "The witches. The Witches of Cascabel."

"Who are they?"

Sofia leaned in, "They told Regina something was not right with Sarah. All that magic she did was bad. They are the ones who are going to help Regina's son, Benny. But now we can ask them about this dead vibora and find out what it is. Maybe *they know. Why was it over Sarah's grave? It has to do with Marianne, I know it. She's always up to no good!"*

Julia huffed in anger, "What's wrong with Regina? And what's wrong with you for not stopping her! She's never told me she goes to see witches. What happened to being a good Catholic? Good Catholics don't deal with witches. She should know better than that."

Sofia cleared her throat. "Well, what would you do? You know the story with her son, Benny. She wants them to fix him. I know you are very set in your ways, but not everything is black and white, Julia. They promised her they could fix him. A new life—away from sin. She wants to see him in the next life. Can you blame her for wanting this? Now, I'll admit, it's not the most conventional thing to do, but under the circumstances I say we fight evil with evil. Let witches deal with witches. It's what God would want."

Julia is quiet for a moment. "Do you think so?"

"Yes. Regina's going to take the boy to them soon. If Sarah hadn't passed away I'm sure the boy would be with them by now. Some town near Laredo. She's going to tell him it's a church retreat but that's where she's taking him. It's a white lie to get rid of this evil."

"She shouldn't lie to the boy. That's not right."

"Well, he shouldn't be gay either," Sofia snapped. "It's the lesser of two evils. God will understand. We really shouldn't be questioning her motives either. We are no one to judge, sister. After all, we should be grateful the Feltons agreed to pay for Sarah's funeral expenses. What were we going to do if they hadn't offered? Do you have that kind of money lying around?"

Julia shook her head. "No. We're barely making it as it is."

"It's not lay-away. You need to pay cash when you bury someone. We should be grateful and supportive to Regina. Besides, she already agreed to buy the house and property once we get Astrid and Marianne out."

"I still don't know how we are going to manage that," said Julia.

"Hector told me Marianne attacked him. I don't know how we're going to get the Devil out of Diller. Regina says these witches, these Witches of Cascabel, are good. They will do what they have to do to help us."

"I suppose." Julia shrugged her shoulders.

"I'll call Regina tonight. Maybe I can even go up with her. Luci has already been with her to see them. She told me Cascabel is about three hours from here. I want to make sure we don't have any problems with Marianne. Or the girl."

"The girl is no trouble, Sofia. She's just a kid. She doesn't have what they have. We would have seen it by now."

Sofia raised her thin left eyebrow, "Remember. It's the little ones that cause the most damage," she said.

I could feel my spirit rage as I saw them head back into their car and out of sight. Why would they think that my mother did anything bad to Benny? She didn't make him gay. Magic doesn't make you gay, and it certainly doesn't take it away. Why would Regina offer to pay for my mother's funeral? They didn't even like each other! I didn't understand why I was seeing any of this!

I wanted out of this state. I needed to go back and talk to Marianne. Maybe I didn't want to be a part of all of this after all. Maybe I am fine not knowing the truth. I was very confused. I needed to get back home. Why did you have to leave me alone, mom? Why did you have to abandon ship? Why am I stuck in this limbo?

I could feel my body—my real body—reacting to my anger. My heart was like a ticking time bomb, a crescendo of rage. Please don't explode! I felt my energy being pulled back towards my body.

Astrid!

Marianne's voice! I saw my real body as it radiated with a multitude of tiny lights. I needed my skin! I needed my eyes! I needed to breathe again! My body was trembling and I could see the worry in Marianne's face.

I soared again. Fast. I propelled through the brush, through the mesquite trees. I needed to return to my body. I needed to calm down. Spirit needed to meet flesh.

Marianne!

Marianne, bring me back!

Astrid, come back. Breathe.

Astrid. Calm down.

Open your eyes. Open your E—

—ASTRID FELT THE GROGGY sensation of revival again. The heaviness made it hard to move but her eyes opened. "Astrid? Astrid? Can you hear me?" Marianne was standing over her. "Sit up slowly, kid," she helped her straighten up.

"I'm fine," whispered Astrid. She cleared her throat and pushed her away weakly. Her heart was still pounding, but it was quickly stabilizing.

"What happened? What did you see? You were trembling. What did you see?"

"I can't do this," said Astrid weakly. "I don't know if I can do that again."

"Astrid, for the love of God, what the hell happened? What did you see?"

Marianne looked into Astrid's eyes and saw a wave of newfound anger stirring, growing. How could she tell her aunt that the witches of Cascabel had been contracted by her best friend's mother? Would she ever look at them in the face again? Could she look at Benny in the face without remembering that his mom started all of this? "This was a mistake," she struggled to lift herself from the ground, and looked up into the midnight sky and said: "Some gift this turned out to be."

Photography

ASTRID SLAMMED HER bedroom door with such force that the picture frames on her walls were jolted out of alignment. The welter of emotions she felt—hatred, resentment, and bewilderment—overwhelmed her. What did all of this mean? Why had she listened to Marianne? Were these visions even real? And if they were, what exactly were they? Could someone truly detach their soul? Was it her soul that had witnessed the Pinched Sisters in the cemetery? Was it merely a trick her mind conjured? Or perhaps a ruse by Marianne? She was awash with uncertainty.

All she could do was try to calm her mind and shake off the tingling sensation that overtook her. It was fear. It was sadness. She hated this feeling. Astrid sat on the side of her bed and took deep breaths, trying to center herself. A tap at the door caused the tingling sensation to subside. The light noise brought her thoughts back into focus.

"Astrid," Marianne called from behind the door.

"Go away," she was too weak to scream, but the door squeaked open. Astrid's eyes darted to the sky when she heard the door open. "I'm fine," she huffed. "You don't need to comfort me. You don't need to come give me a pep talk or anything. I'm fine."

"I'm not here to coddle you," said Marianne. "I'm here to make sure you are safe."

"I'm safe," she repeated dryly.

Marianne crossed her arms across her chest and stared at Astrid for a moment before breaking the silence. "You have your mother's hair."

Astrid cringed at the comment then brushed her hair back. "That's a fascinating observation, Marianne. Way to dismiss the elephant in the room."

She picked up a camera on Astrid's desk. "You like taking pictures?" Marianne asked.

Astrid shrugged her shoulders.

"I used to like taking pictures, too."

"Pictures are truth," she said.

"There is no truth," Marianne remarked. "Everything is subjective."

"Pictures *are* truth. They capture a moment."

"You think because you can record a moment in a photograph that you have any idea of what the truth really is? I have seen things that cannot be explained in the mind and cannot be captured on film, does it mean they don't exist?"

"Sooo Deep," Astrid muttered and rolled her eyes.

Marianne scoffed. "You have stepped outside of your skin. You have seen things which have obviously upset you. You have the nerve to say the things we see with our own eyes are black and white. You're better than that, Astrid."

"I always thought you could capture a moment. That's why I like taking pictures. I always feel like an outsider looking in. I don't tell anyone these things. But I feel different, out of place. I feel like taking pictures somehow makes me part of the equation. If I hadn't been there to snap a moment or capture an event, I never would have existed. Do you know what I mean?"

"I do," she said. "It makes sense. You're part of the world that lives on labels and likes compartments."

She nodded. "I guess so."

Marianne leaned in: "What exactly did you see that made you so angry? What did you see tonight?"

"I saw Sophia and Julia in the cemetery."

"At this hour?"

"They found a dead Malinal snake. Julia was making sure it was real. They said that Regina went to see the Witches of Cascabel. I heard them. Luci took her. She must have sent them. She must be the reason mom's dead."

Marianne was quiet for a moment. "Regina has no idea who she's dealing with. She's in trouble."

"Trouble? Trouble! Good! I'm glad she's in trouble! Then Sophia and Julia said they were glad that Regina went to the witches. They said they were going to visit them as well so they could get rid of you and me. To get us out of this house." Astrid was crying now. "How am I going to face them again? How am I going to face the Feltons? Benny? He's my best friend."

"You have to calm down. You can't let on that you know any of this. Regina might run back to them if she feels cornered. The last thing we need is for Sophia and Julia to visit them as well. When they find out who we are, the daughters of Carmen Cortez, they will be in for a world of trouble themselves. We need to find out what exactly Regina has done and what they are planning to do next. It would be best if you rested so you can ride the wind again. Tomorrow. They'll all be meeting again at the Felton Rose. You can try to see what else you can find out. I know that you are mad at your friend, but you've got to go see if you can find out anything about this, Astrid." She pulled her niece's head up. "Please look at me."

"Waking up is painful."

"I know. But the more you practice, the less painful it is going to be."

"It feels wrong."

"How can it be wrong when we're trying to solve a mystery."

"We don't know for sure if Regina really did send them. It could all be a coincidence," said Astrid. "Maybe I'm jumping to the wrong conclusion, misinterpreting the picture. Maybe Julia and Sophia are trying to help."

"Oh, Astrid. You have no idea of what people are truly capable of…" her voice drifted.

"Even my own family?"

"Especially our family."

Taxes, Death and Benny Felton

EARLY THE NEXT MORNING, Astrid made her way back to the cemetery. She didn't bother telling Marianne where she was going, a little part of her felt that her aunt would already know. Being at the graveyard was strangely reassuring. Even under the dreary, gray clouds and periodic sprinkles, being in the cemetery was more pleasant than being at home with her thoughts. After her grandmother passed away, she often visited her grandmother's gravesite and found it comforting. She couldn't understand how people could be afraid of cemeteries. Her grandmother's words came back to her: "Don't fear the dead, only the living can hurt you."

Sarah's headstone was located near the end of the cemetery, facing a brushy area along a cliff overlooking the Rio Grande River. The mud made it difficult to navigate the scattered old headstones and small grave houses.

She remembered the last time she mentioned going to the cemetery to Benny. "You're like a psycho," Benny hissed. "Why would anyone visit a cemetery alone? That's odd... even for you."

"It's not odd. It's actually very calming. Intimate, really."

"Jeez, it's not a date, Astrid. It's a burial ground."

"I don't know about that. I think it is kind of like a date. A date with your loved one. A quiet meeting. The dead can't come to you, so you have to go to them."

"You are so weird."

"It's very peaceful. Not everything has to be flashy and over-the-top to be important. Sometimes things can be quiet, comforting and peaceful."

"Too peaceful if you ask me."

"It's kind of poetic. It's my way of being alone with my grandma while everyone is asleep, the living and the dead."

"That gives me the creeps," he shuddered.

"Your hair color you use gives a lot of people the creeps, but you still wear it. I don't bash your choices."

"Girl, just be careful. There are lots of psychos out there. I've never heard of good things happening in a cemetery."

"I'll be fine, Benny. The last time I was there I was on the white fence surrounding my granny's grave. It was a full moon so I could see everything. It wasn't dark at all but one of the solar lights on the fence post suddenly went off. I was about to fix it when an owl landed next to the street lamp. It looked like a baby. The little thing was covered in white and beige feathers and for the longest time it just stared at me. I felt so at peace, Benny. I felt so humbled. I remember my granny telling me about how spirits become owls. I think she visited me that night. I took out my camera, you know I always have my camera with me, and I was about to snap a photo when it flew off. It had such a wide wingspan. I wasn't expecting something so small to have such huge wings. I think it was a way for my granny to let me know everything was OK."

Her family was one of the only ones to decorate their loved ones' graves with cemetery lights. They took pride in keeping her grandmother's gravesite neat and colorful. Astrid hated to admit it, but she never saw a purpose in tending to and decorating graves. She thought it was a waste of time, an unnecessary anchor of her heritage. With her mother buried next to her grandmother, she decided bringing offerings and items meant to commemorate Sarah's life wasn't such a bad idea.

Several flower arrangements surrounded the mound of dirt over Sarah's grave. Astrid opened the little wooden gate to the fence encompassing her mom and grandma's graves and closed it behind her. She was in a good place, she was with her family now.

"Mom," Astrid ran her hair through her fingers. "I want to say I'm sorry I'm such a mess. You were probably looking down at me shaking your head wanting to smack the living hell out of me. I can already hear you saying, 'It's bad enough these people talk about us. Do you have to give them another reason? Really?' I am sorry, mom. I honestly am. But I don't understand any of this. You're supposed to be here with me. You're supposed to be home with me. You downstairs reading or watching television. Me upstairs listening to music, editing photos at the same time. Why is Marianne here and not you? I'm worried about the Pinched Sisters. They want the house, and they want to send us off. But where am I supposed to go? I don't have anyone else. Maybe just Marianne, but she's the weirdest one of all, and that's saying a lot." Astrid paused. "Why didn't you tell me about her? She says you spoke a lot. Why didn't you ever mention her at least? About the things she can do. I've never seen the Pinched Sisters look so scared," she chuckled a bit. "It's the same way they used to look at grandma. They knew she was more powerful than they ever could be. Even in old age, she was still more powerful than they were. Why didn't you tell me, mom? Why didn't you tell me things I should have known?"

She stood in silence for a moment, then felt her phone vibrate. She had been avoiding Benny's several texts, but she knew it was him the minute she felt the buzz.

The text read: **Are you OK?**

Astrid exhaled sharply. She didn't feel like dealing with Benny, but she knew it was a matter of time before they needed to speak.

Reluctantly, she replied: **At the cemetery.**

A few seconds later he wrote: **Stay there. Heading over.**

She put her phone back in her pocket. Astrid didn't want to deal with Benny, but resigned to the idea. How can you avoid the taxes, death or Benny Felton? In time, they all eventually find you.

Thorns at The Rose

BENNY HAD BEEN looking for Astrid all night. He was expecting her at the *Novenario*. It was strange seeing Astrid's relatives gathered in his living room, saying prayers and devotions for his best friend's mother without seeing her there. Even more strange was seeing how his mother greeted everyone with such tenderness. He almost choked on his own laughter when he heard her tell the ladies what good friends she and Sarah were.

"And since when were you all friends," Benny asked as soon as the guests had left.

"Shouldn't you be getting ready for bed? You've got school tomorrow," she replied.

"How many more nights of this are we going to have to go through?"

"Nine," she said. "*Novenarios* are nine days."

"What is this anyway? I know it's like a prayer, but what's it for?"

"It's to ask God for mercy when judging those who have passed."

"So you're praying she gets into heaven? You're asking God to let Sarah into the pearly gates."

"Well," she said with the hint of a smirk on her face, "We can try."

"You don't think we should have Astrid here? Don't you think God would listen more if the daughter were making these requests? It's not right. Do you think Sarah was a bad person who needs our intervention?"

"Well, I don't know why she's not here. Her aunts asked her to be here. Maybe she isn't up for this. Some people handle death in their own ways. As for Sarah, we all have our secrets. It doesn't hurt to pray for the dead."

"Astrid's not answering her phone, like at all. I don't know what's up with her."

"We can only do so much. We've helped that family out as much as we can. You know very well that our family has always supported them. I know what a good friend you have been to her. This is how she pays you back? Not even a text. If I were her, I'd be texting you to let you know that I was safe. It's very selfish of her. After all, you've been through with her. I mean, my God, we even paid for her mother's funeral. I would think she would be here as a thank you. Not even to thank me, to thank you as her friend."

"You paid for Sarah's funeral?"

Regina nodded slowly. "Julia and Sophia said they couldn't afford it, and the other aunt of hers is a misfit. That degenerate Marianne. God knows what her financial situation is. So yes. We stepped in. Your father said he would take care of it. I was there when he wrote the check. You know very well we're not doing as well financially as we used to be. Even with selling the land on Bridgman Road. What did we get for that except more taxes? But the people expected our help, so we stepped up. That's what Felton's do."

Benny nodded his head. "That was very nice of you." He crossed his arms and smiled. "That was special, mom. I'm really proud of you."

"Am I still the Forth Gorgon Sister," she asked, raising her eyebrow.

Benny smiled coyly. "No. You're not."

Back in his room, Benny felt a sense of relief in seeing Astrid's reply flash on his phone's screen. He puts his phone in his pants pocket, makes his way downstairs, and finds Regina sitting at the kitchen table.

Regina smiled at him. "Morning." she chirped in delight.

"Morning, are you having another *novenario* here tonight?"

"I told you yesterday; it's nine days. So, yes, silly boy."

"OK. I finally got a hold of Astrid. I'm going to ask her to come today."

"Oh," said Regina, turning to Luci, who had just entered the kitchen. "Well, maybe she'll come today. I hope she knows the Rose is always welcome to her. Our house is open if they want to come."

"I'll make her come. She has to be here. No question about it." Regina waited until Benny was out of the home before giving Luci a stern glare.

"Did you do what I asked you to do?"

"She didn't come, did she?"

Regina bit her lower lip and squinted her eyes as if processing a thought, "She and the aunt should stay away." Regina looked outside and noticed a light rain falling in the backyard. "It's going to be an ugly day."

"It's a cold front. They said it was going to rain all week."

"Yes. My bones were aching this morning," Regina sighed. "When did we get this old," she whispered, not expecting a reply.

"About ten years ago," replied Luci with a smirk on her face.

Regina shot her big eyes at Luci. "It's all downhill after fifty," she said wryly. "God, I hate this weather. Look at how gray it looks outside. It's like the world is in mourning."

"Aren't we in mourning?" asked Luci.

"Well," she muttered. "Well, yes."

"Maybe the weather is just reflecting our sadness."

"And since when did you become so philosophical? What have you got to be sad about? You didn't really even know Sarah all that well."

"She was a good woman. We were friends. You should be even sadder. You all grew up together."

"Why would I cry over her?"

Luci cleaned the kitchen table.

"We weren't family," said Regina.

"You were raised together, no? In this little village, I imagined you formed a bond with people. Small communities tend to make people stick together."

"Of course we do, what a thing to say. That doesn't mean I'm going to have a breakdown every time someone I've met throughout my life dies. I'm just not an emotional person."

"I've heard you crying plenty of times in the bathroom. I know Benny makes you cry."

"What child doesn't cut into a mother."

"You have emotions, *Señora* Regina. Why don't you feel anything about Sarah?"

"Luci, what has gotten into you?" She set her coffee down. "Is there

150

something you want to tell me?"

"What do you mean?"

"You shouldn't be speaking to me like that."

"Ah, I'm sorry, *Señora* Regina. I thought over the years we had become more familiar. I thought you were my friend. I thought that's why I went with you to see those *brujas*. I thought we were close. I thought you confided in me."

Regina tensed and stiffened her back, "What are you getting at, Luci? I don't like where this is going."

"It never occurred to me to question you," began Luci, her voice was lower and quite tense. "When you said that all I had to do was drive you into Laredo. You said you were too afraid to go by yourself. I didn't mind waiting for you in the car because you've been very good to me–I acknowledge that. I can't get some questions out of my head though. I've had them in my head all night."

Regina exhaled heavily and scoffed.

"Luci, you don't know what you're talking about. Maybe you need a day off."

"You had something with you when you left the witch's house. You went in empty-handed and you came out with a suitcase," she said. "You put it in the back of my car."

Regina clenched her jaw, her eyes widened with fury.

Luci continued, "You were very nervous when we came back home from that trip. I kept looking at the rear-view mirror. Guilty. You looked very guilty. What did you have in that case, *Señora*? Why haven't you cried for an old friend? Why do you not want me to tell anyone about our trip to see the Witches of Cascabel? Why do you want to keep the girl away from here?"

Regina stood up slowly from her chair. "Be very careful about who you start talking to, Luci. Your daughter's very sick. If a perfectly healthy woman can drop dead in a day without anyone batting an eyelash, can you imagine the fuss anyone would make over a real sick person?"

Luci nodded and grabbed a jacket from the kitchen chair and put it on. "You really *would* hurt my child, wouldn't you? Sarah didn't make your son gay, *Señora*. It wasn't magic that made him that way. It was God. God forgive me for helping you do what you did."

"I'd do anything in the world to save my son!" Regina pounded on the table.

"Your son is not in danger, *Señora*. There's nothing wrong with him."

"He's been poisoned!" She pounded her fist harder this time, causing her coffee cup to tremble.

Luci felt Regina's burning eyes stare her down as she walked across the kitchen to the back door. She shook her head weakly before saying, "The only one filled with poison in this house is you, Regina."

Benny and Astrid

ASTRID'S GAZE DRIFTED upwards as she sat on a cement bench near her mother's grave. The drizzle had stopped, making way for a pleasant sun. She could hear birds in the distance and the wind made the chimes hanging on a nearby tree sing. A pair of red robins perched on a nearby tree.

"It's almost insulting that I should have to look at a sky like this," said Astrid to the wind.

She followed a small car driving up to the cemetery. A few seconds later, Benny appeared and started walking towards her.

"How's it going?" He gave her a hug.

"I've been better," she avoided looking at him. "I like the weather, though."

"Yeah," said Benny. "It was really bad this morning. I think it's going to be a nice day."

"Days are rarely nice anymore," she kicked little pebbles in the ground and was silent for a moment. "So what do you want?"

"What do you mean, what do I want? I came to check up on you. Is your phone not working? I've been texting you since last night."

"Service has been crappy," she lied, still avoiding his eyes.

"Why didn't you make it to the *novenario*? I assumed you would be there. Surprise-surprise, you weren't there."

"I didn't even know there was going to be one until last night." She thought for a moment and decided not to mention the fact that Luci had warned her not to go. "Why don't you ask your mother?"

"My mother? She's the one who offered you our house. Your aunts said

153

they invited you. It was expected that you'd be there. She told me."

"And you believed her? Of all the lies your mom has told you, this is the one you decide to believe?"

"She hasn't been lying to me. She's been very good to your family. You might show a little gratitude to her. To *me*."

"Benny, she's been lying to you her whole life."

"Look, I know you're upset. You don't need to be like this. I was asking why you didn't go. If you don't want to honor your mother, it's on you."

"Honor my mother?" She said loudly, in a how-dare-you tone before scoffing. She was about to scream, about to explode, about to tell him that his mother caused this. "I'm in a fucking cemetery. I'm standing over my mother's grave. How dare you say I'm not honoring my mother."

"Why are you acting so weird?"

"I'm not acting weird. You're the one acting weird. You've always been a freak."

He snapped his fingers at her, "Girl, I am nothing but fabulousness."

"Oh, Benny, shut the hell up. Enough of that 'I'm fabulous nonsense.' We both know you don't mean it. You're always bitching about how that psycho mother of yours treats you like shit. Stop pretending. Get out of your bubble, dude. You're just a broken clown with mommy issues. Some of us have real problems. I don't have a fucking mom anymore, and you're giving me crap because I didn't go to your house," her voice trailed. "Look. I don't have time for this. Go put on a show for someone else. I have more important things to do."

Astrid was too angry to realize Marianne had pulled up to the cemetery and was suddenly staring at them. She broke the tension by clearing her throat. "I figured you'd be here. Why didn't you tell me you were coming? What's going on here, Astrid?"

"Nothing," she rose from a slab, "Benny was just leaving for school."

"Is this the Felton boy?" she pointed at Benny.

Benny crossed his arms. "The one and only. I'm today's human punching bag apparently."

"You look like your dad," said Marianne, pulling out a cigarette from her pocket.

"Who are you?" he said, almost immediately regretting his snippy tone.

Marianne blew a puff of smoke towards him. "I'm the wise, mentally unstable aunt, kid. Don't use that tone with me again or I'll rearrange your face so you go from fairy to frog real quick."

After a moment of stunned silence, Benny grimaced and said, "Whatever, I just came to check up on Astrid. I'm just trying to be a good friend. You remember what that is, right Astrid?"

Astrid turned away, dusting off her jeans.

"People's good deeds really ARE written in water," muttered Benny before storming out of the cemetery.

Marianne turned to her niece. "There's something very odd about that boy. What was that about?"

"I don't know. He was probably quoting Shakespeare. He's always quoting—" she raised her hands in exasperation, "You know what? I don't even care. We have more pressing matters at hand. I need to find out more about why they sent the Malinal snakes."

She pointed to a barrel at the end of the cemetery.

"What's in there?"

"I saw it last night," said Astrid. "I saw Julia and Sophia come here."

"At night? That doesn't sound like them."

"I know. But I heard them talking about a snake and I saw it for myself. It's in there. The body of a Malinal. Do you think you can use it to find out who sent it?"

"I can't do that."

"Oh," Astrid lowered her head. "I thought there was a spell we could do. Use it to find out more about this whole mess."

"Take me to the snake. I want to make sure of what we are dealing with."

MARIANNE LIFTED THE BODY with a tree branch. The snake was now stiff, covered in black ants that scattered as it hit the ground.

"It's heavier than I thought," said Marianne, tossing the stick out of sight.

Astrid bent closer. "Jesus. It almost looks black now. But some of the rattle has come off."

"Yeah," said Marianne. "I've seen these before."

"Then it *is* a Malinal Snake. Someone sent it to hurt my mother."

"It was sent to find magic, that's for sure. Whether or not it was sent to hurt your mother specifically, we don't really know."

Astrid felt a rage form at the pit of her stomach. She stared down at the decaying carcass wanting nothing more than to crush it even more. Snakes had always disgusted her, she wanted nothing more than to pulverize the scales, collagen, and meat. Pound every inch of it into the ground. Make it disappear. Put the beast where it had put her mother. Astrid was afraid of snakes, but this one, this terrible worm with teeth, was not something she feared. A strange bravery had taken over. At that moment, she could have faced a thousand Malinal snakes and not feel her pulse rise even a little. A static grew from this rage, similar to what she had experienced when she rode the wind. This time, it was a heat that rose from within her core, and she felt her body begin to tremble.

"Marianne," she said concerned. "Something's wrong." She extended her arms and felt her hands pulsate.

"What is it?"

As if the ground had grabbed hold of her, she felt her feet tensing up. Almost immediately, the snake's tail began to jerk. A little at first and then more aggressively. The blue rattle began moving on its own. It made a terrible, hissing sound.

"Why is it doing that?" Astrid asked, bewildered.

Taking a step closer, Marianne lifted her sunglasses. "I'm not sure."

"Be careful! I think it's still alive. It's still moving."

Marianne said, "No. I think it's you, Astrid. I think you're moving it."

Astrid felt the heat from her core intensify, and the snake's head began rising slowly.

"My God," said Marianne. "How are you doing that?"

Astrid turned to her aunt, her eyes wide and frightened. "I'm not doing anything, what is this?" Astrid looked back at the animal. It appeared to be in a strange trance.

"Astrid," Marianne shouted to her niece, but she was unable to take her gaze from the serpent. "Astrid!" Marianne shrieked, causing her to turn from the snake. Its head fell to the floor.

Astrid was brought to her knees, tears streaming down her face. "What is wrong with me?" She looked pleadingly at her aunt.

Marianne knelt next to Astrid and touched her face. Astrid fell into her arms and began heavily sobbing. "Shh. It's going to be okay," said Marianne as she attempted to comfort her niece. "Listen to me Astrid, your power can be a curse, but it can also be a blessing." Marianne kissed the top of her head. "Even the chosen must know pain."

Toxica

BENNY COULDN'T CONCENTRATE. He could not release the anger and resentment coursing through him. How could Astrid treat him so badly? He was only trying to help. Only ever trying to be a good friend to her. Benny arrived home and immediately retreated to his bedroom. He could not bear the idea of telling his mother. He did not want to see the stupid smirk on her face. The "I told you so" would brighten up her whole aura. His mind was filled with emotions that he had never felt before. He was hurt, angry, and full of turmoil.

Benny sat at his desk, pondering what to say to Astrid. Would she even bother reading it? Did she need time to cool off? What had gotten into her? A few months prior, he might have sought a destructive distraction, anything to still his nerves. Instead of confronting his sadness, he had taken to cutting himself, yearning to feel anything—even pain—over the engulfing gloom. But he didn't keep those tiny razors anymore; he had promised himself he'd stop. The counselors made him feel awkward too. Their prying attention only compounded his anguish. Usually, he'd confide in Astrid during such moments. She had a knack for pulling him from the brink. But how could he turn to her when she was now the very source of his turmoil? Typically, Regina was the cause of his distress. He paused, reflecting, "Why did Mom agree to pay for the funeral?" The decision felt off. His mother was far from compassionate; every mention of Astrid would earn him a reprimand. She had even banned their friendship a few months ago. Something was amiss, a poison seeping into the situation. From his closet, he pulled out a shirt he'd been reserving for a special moment. Though he couldn't explain it, he felt that now was the time to let the shirt convey his emotions.

He heard a knocking at his door and his mother's head poked inside. "People are going to get here at seven. I need your help tonight. Luci can't make it. I need your help serve any guests."

Benny did not reply.

"Did you hear me? I need your help."

"Astrid said you didn't invite her," he said.

"Benny. I don't have time for this right now. That's ridiculous. This is meant to honor her mother. Why wouldn't I invite her?"

"Why would she lie?"

"Maybe because she comes from a family of liars."

"Sarah wasn't a liar. She was a good woman."

Regina rolled her eyes. "A good woman? OK. I'll keep my mouth quiet because I don't want to speak ill of the dead. Especially if I'm honoring them in my own house."

"Why *are* you doing it here?"

"What?"

"The *novenario*. Shouldn't Astrid be doing this at her house? It's weird. It doesn't make any sense, mom."

"Their house is too small."

"Bruh, only six old ladies showed up yesterday. I think they thought the *novenario* was for them. How much room do six people need?"

"What's your point?"

"The point is that it's weird. Why would you do this? Why isn't Astrid here? This is for her mom. Why are you taking over the show? Is this a show?"

"Her sisters asked me to have it here. I'm just helping a friend."

"Why?"

"I told you their house is too small."

"There's something else. This isn't like you. You didn't even like Sarah. I know you didn't."

"You don't know what I think," said Regina.

"I know you think she turned me gay. You tell me that every chance you get."

She tightened her shoulders. "You are NOT like that. Stop saying things like that. I know you only tell me those things to try and upset me." She stopped to look at his shirt, looked away, then pointed at it. Regina took a deep angry breath. "Benjamin Lee Felton, you take off that shirt right now."

"Why?"

"You know very well why."

"It's just a shirt."

"It has the word TOXICA on it. You think you're trying to be funny?"

"So?"

"You're not a girl."

"I'm not saying I'm a girl. It's not intended to represent me."

"Then what's the point of wearing it?"

"It's supposed to be you. See?" He pointed at his chest. "It's even carrying a little crown. Got your curly hair."

"*Quitatelo!* Take it off NOW!"

"No!"

"Take it the hell OFF," she yelled, forcing him against the door. Regina pierced at Benny with cold, red eyes. "After everything I've done for you," she sneered. "Ungrateful little shit!"

"No one asked you to try to fix me. You can't even fix yourself."

He pushed her back but rage propelled her forward. She slapped him across the face. The force was meant to show him who ran the show. Regina expected him to cower back, to fly into hysterics and cry on the floor. But the boy stood and stared her square in the eyes in disbelief and disgust. "You Psycho BITCH," he roared.

Regina stormed out of the room and slammed his door shut. "Don't come out of there!" she screamed. "You just wait until your father comes! I can't believe you! After all I've done! The things I've done for love." She pounded on the door. "You stay the hell in there!"

Regina stormed into her bathroom and tried to calm herself down. Five minutes later, she looked at herself in the mirror. Her hands were still trembling as she applied her lipstick.

Misery At The Rose

A T SUNDOWN, ASTRID and Marianne made their way back into the altar room. This time, Marianne sat Astrid in the middle of the room and told her she was on her own. Marianne would not guide her. She would not always have someone telling her to focus, relax, breathe and release. Astrid needed to ride the wind on her own, but she felt comfort knowing her aunt was watching over her as she did.

She closed her eyes and felt her mind go dark. It took a while to relax. Astrid kept hearing the sounds of birds in the distance. A good ten minutes was what it took for her to get comfortable enough not to notice her surroundings. The smells of the room. The rustling of trees outside. It's not easy to escape the reality of your mind, the dangers of your thoughts. Yet something happened to Astrid, and it was almost instantaneous, like a switch was turned on. The alter room was new now, vivid with colors and static. This was her new reality. The magic welcome her in on its own, it easily and reassuringly let its pulse and vibrations bathe her. Sure, it was difficult without hearing Marianne reassure her, but eventually, she felt the familiar tingling in her arms. The cold energy traveling up to her chest and down her thighs to the tips of her toes. She was static energy once more, and this meant she was free. This meant she was not bound to her skin anymore. She was ready to ride the wind.

TO THE FELTON ROSE, that's where I'll go. Marianne is by my body watching

161

over me. I know I am safe. I rose above the town effortlessly, weightless. It's amazing to detach from reality. To split from the flesh. My spirit has tasted freedom, and it's eager to experience more.

The most prominent house in all of Diller is calling me. It's not too far from my home and I've been there countless other times, but this time I don't know the house's energy. I don't know. Something about the way it vibrates makes me uneasy. It's always such a peaceful house, its washed-out pink Victorian exterior has lost its luster. The Rose was no longer in full bloom.

Where was everyone? No cars were parked on the driveway. No one was greeting people at the door. No Pinched Sisters. The Rose was supposed to be filled with people praying for my mother, but this place was void of all life.

I entered through the North, through the large entrance with the great porch. My grandmother told me it had been designed by Benny's great-grandfather as a present for his wife (Matilde.) They said it was designed by a French architect named Gaspar. It was photographed by a magazine. She showed me a newspaper clipping about it once.

I passed through the door. A heaviness had overtaken the house, one which had grown over time. One I never noticed before. I could sense this energy was penetrated in the floorboards and ornate crown molding of the old house. It spread slowly, but had spread its tentacles across the base of the old home. I hate the word 'cancerous', but it's the only way to describe it. It was not placed here by anyone or anything. This was a malady made by the Feltons. It's different in the real world. I could not see the gray hue of death and mourning outside of this state. For all of its beauty and its prestige, the Felton Rose is a grave house.

I saw Benny's father, George, sitting at the dining room table. He's still in his police uniform. Benny looks an awful lot like his father, which is good, but age has not been kind to him. He looks much older than he should, the consequence of marrying such a vile woman. The sun spots on the entirety of his face which could be mistaken for freckles. His eyelids have become hooded, and the beard he's been growing since No-Shave November has become more gray than black.

Regina enters the dining room in an over-sized plush, red bathrobe. She is haggard, appearing much older than her husband. I can tell she has been crying, the skin around her eyes is dark. They are engorged, her eyes are bloodshot. Two coffee cups are set on the table.

*Regina is seated next to George She clears her throat: "I never wanted to do this,"
she whispered, her voice almost quivering. I don't know how sincere her tone is.
I've never known this woman to be anything other than a living stone. "You make
it seem like this was all planned or something." She pauses, her attention turns to
George, but he seemed lost in his own world. "That's why I had to send everyone
home. He attacked me. Ungrateful little shit! You should have seen the way he
yelled at me. Then Luci quit. How's that for a slap in the face, huh? We helped that
pinche mojada get her papers in order and this is how she pays us back. That's
what we get for helping a wetback."*

*Regina takes a deep breath then raises her voice. "Can't you understand that I'm
sending him there to help him? I'm doing what any other mother in my position
would do. I mean, if this was happening to me, I would want my mother to do
something about it. It's like a disease, George. He's ill! We need to make him better."*

*George remained silent, his eyes fixed on a spot on the wall. He wanted to be
anywhere but here. He was prepared for an endless silence.*

*Regina abruptly pounded the table, causing some coffee to spill. "Say something!"
She was screaming now. The vibrations of the house became stronger. I feel them
pulsing through me. "Say something for the love of God. What the hell are you good
for if you can't even support me in this?"*

*George turned to look at her. "I don't think this will help him, Gina. You don't
even know those people. You should have asked me first."*

*"So we should have let him do the things he does? Have him parade around in
makeup! Continue sneaking up boys to his room while we're not here. This is your
fault. You never stepped up. You never showed him how to be a man."*

George was silent again.

*She stood up, crossed her arms around her chest. "You know this wouldn't have
happened if your father were alive. He would have set him right. He wouldn't have
let this show go on for as long as it has. The hair, the clothing, and now that boy he
had in his room. Under our very noses, George! In this very house! No-no-no-no.
Your father would have done something. It's the truth and you know it. Jesus, it's
like you don't even care about him! He's your son. Don't you have any compassion
for him? Don't you know what the world is saying about him? About us!"*

George picked up the coffee, sipped it quietly for a moment before speaking again. "He told me the other day that he didn't pick me."

"George, what the hell are you talking about?"

He cleared his throat. I never realized how slowly he speaks. "It was something Sarah once told him before she—"

"Died," Regina said with a disgusted look on her face.

"Passed away," George replied. "Apparently they had a conversation about choosing parents one time. He was complaining about us. Apparently she told him that he chose us. Before he was born his soul had a choice and he chose us."

"Bologna," said Regina.

George dismissed her comment and continued. "He said he didn't believe her because he would have never picked an asshole like me." A redness overtakes his face as his eyes well up with tears. "Well, that works both ways, I suppose. I know I should love him—and I do, I really, really do—but I don't think I would have picked him either. If they lined up 100 different boys, all of them in a single file, shoulder to shoulder, and I had to pick the one would not have been Benny. Not by a long shot."

As Regina's frown softened, a tear fell from her eye.

"I don't know him, Gina. I don't think I ever did. I don't think I ever will."

Regina shook her head, "Well, I still love our boy."

George lowered his head, "I love him, too! I will always love him. I don't know who he is. I don't like that at all. I don't think I can love all of him. Not all of him."

She crouched down next to him. "Then I did the right thing. I did the right thing, and in no time at all, he'll be back. It will be like this never happened," she cries. "We can forget. It's easy to forget. It's the easiest thing in the world," she reached for his forehead and kissed it. Tears streamed down her face, wetting the top of his head. "You'll see. We did the right thing. We did it for him. We did it for us. It's the only choice we have."

George glanced away. "I guess we'll find out in a week. Let's hope you are right about all of this."

I can't believe what I am seeing. I can't understand how these two parents can be so blind to the fact that their son is special, unique. Yes, he is dopey and nosey, yes, he is self-centered and egotistical, a whirlwind of contradictions—a boy in a girl

164

in a boy in a girl. A decent human—those are hard to come by these days. A pure soul with a complicated mind. What is wrong with them? Where is Benny in all of this? Poor Benny, I shouldn't have thought he was such a jerk. These people are the jerks. He's harmless, and with parents like these, who wouldn't prefer the company of drama. It's easy to escape into the drama of life when your reality is so utterly depressing. Who doesn't need gossip and stories when the reality of their lives is so desperately bleak. The ridiculous cliches of hatred.

I rise past the dining room up the stairs to the first door to the left into Benny's room. It's dimly lit, the pulse of his bedroom is weak. There is life, but it is in a fragile state.

Something about being in this state, in this colorful, mirrored realm, heightened my senses. I couldn't tell what Benny was thinking, not even close, but I could see the trembling of his lips and the pain in his eyes. I could smell the sadness. I hear the heaviness of his chest, the way his lungs pump more than just air. They carry a heavy fog. A dense and malignant form of anger. A queer breed of fury, isolation and despair. I know exactly what he is; he is broken. I am looking at a spirit that had been chipped away, bleeding primordial ooze, weeping solitude and regret. I want to hold him. I want to share the love I have for him, to let him and everyone I know that I adore and care so much for this tall, blue-haired weirdo. I am more than proud to call him my friend—I am honored.

I inch closer to see him in a deep writing trance. It always fascinates me when Benny writes because he has the best penmanship of anyone I know. He is excellent at forging signatures—Lord knows the countless times I (and many other students) have asked him to reproduce their parent's name on permission slips or homework assignments. He writes with delicacy and lots of loops, but the pen he holds looks heavy and the ink doesn't sing. It weeps.

"I am," he writes, then stops abruptly, turning to the side. For a moment, he stares right at me. At least it feels that way. Could he see me? Could he feel me? I don't know, but I see his eyes fill with tears. There is pain, so much pain in those eyes. I wouldn't wish such a pain on anyone—not even those damned Pinched Sisters. "Benny," I whisper, hoping he can hear my voice. He turns away and continues moving the pen.

"I know I stand out. I see the wide eyes when I walk into a room. I know my color clashes with the decor. I am not meant for the display case I've been placed in. I've tried to censor the offensiveness. There was a time I tried to hide and the world seemed like a better place. That story got old quickly. The gay experience is written, I guess. We are weeds in a garden waiting to be plucked out. Can I imagine what it's like to think of a future where you have to tell your parents you met the love of your life and have it turn into some ridiculous circus? No "congratulations," just a bunch of tears and "where did I go wrong?" It wouldn't be so offensive if it was a moral issue. Oh no, these people bring it to the next level and claim they hate it because they want to save my immortal soul. I'm tired. I'm hungry for more. My heart is not at peace.

I am tired of fighting a cancer that doesn't exist. I am tired of mending a heart that hasn't even known true love. I can't protect an innocent soul. But most of all, I'm tired of being an embarrassment to you and myself. I am a lie both inside and out. I love you both, but I can't perform anymore. I know my lines but don't know the role. How terrible and how exhausting it is to be on stage but never seen.

—Nay, weep not, gentle Eros. There is left us Ourselves to end ourselves.

—Shakespeare."

He sets down the pen and reaches for a vibrant blue box the size of a small crate under his desk and places it on top. Benny opens the box slowly, revealing a photo album inside and takes a moment to peruse the photos before carefully pulling out a small, hand-held gun. His hands tremble slightly as he holds the weapon, his eyes fixed on the object of his fascination.

My spirit goes wild. "Benny! Benny, NO!"

He stares at the weapon in a grim, horrible manner. It is the miserable look of false salvation.

"Benny, DON'T!"

I reach for the gun and swing right through it.

"Benny, don't you even think about it!"

I feel my body, my real body—the one being guarded by Marianne, turning hot and the thumping of my heart intensified. I heard the echo of my aunt faintly calling to me. "It's been too long. Come back."

Suddenly, a familiar blue snake emerged from the window, its scales glinting in the light. It slithered through a small opening, and I could feel its presence. The snake seemed to sense my gaze, and it rattled its tail in warning, sending vibrations that shook my world. My vision blurred, but Benny didn't seem to notice. He was transfixed by the gun in his hands, his eyes wide with manic thoughts.

I scream, "It's by the window. Turn to the window! It's coming. Benny! The snake!"

"Astrid, come back," *Marianne's voice is a clap of distant thunder.*

I can't come back! Don't you see Benny needs me? He's going to be attacked!

"I have to," *the thunder roars again.*

No.

He needs me!

"Astrid, I have to—" *my aunt's voice echos all around me.*

"Benny! Benny pl—"

Highly Blessed

ASTRID FELT THE weight of her energy rush back into her body, but this time, she was too alert and upset to oblige its heaviness. She knew it would take time for her strength to return, but Benny needed her now. Astrid felt her aunt's arms help her off the ground and willed her body back to life. She had to be strong for Benny and rush to his side to help him.

"Let go," Astrid struggled to speak, she knew she had to muster all of her strength to save Benny. "Let go. We have—"

"Calm down!" Marianne held her tightly. "You need to calm down. Astrid, I can see your heart pounding."

"Noooooooooooo! I need to SAVE HIM!" Astrid let out a blood-curdling scream and the walls of the altar room trembled.

Marianne's eyes widened as little plumes of dust rose from the old altar. "Oh my God," she whispered.

Marianne held Astrid tightly, her body trembling with emotion. She could feel the desperation in Astrid's voice, and knew that they had to act quickly. "We have to save him, Marianne," Astrid pleaded. "Benny is going to hurt himself. We don't have much time. I know what he's going to do. Benny! We have to get to him now!" she cried out, her voice filled with urgency. Marianne nodded, and they both ran towards Benny, determined to save him from himself.

Marianne kissed the top of Astrid's damp forehead, took a deep breath then nodded. "The Felton Rose,"she whispered, then helped Astrid to her feet. A surge of Adrenalin entered Astrid's body and she felt her feet fly out the door.

Marianne's car sped towards Benny's home. The house was less than a mile away, but it felt like an eternity. Astrid flung the car door open and quickly dashed towards the Felton Rose. Her heartbeat had never been so rapid, not even when she ran towards the cemetery after her mother died. This was the run of her life. She had no time to spare. Astrid needed to run past the Feltons, run up the stairs and stop Benny from doing the unthinkable.

Astrid banged on the door. "Let me in!"

The porch light turned on moments later. A visibly shaken George Felton greeted her at the door. "Astrid," he said, "What's going on? What the hell is going on here!"

"Please," cried Astrid, "Let me in. I need to see Benny!"

"Astrid, it's late," his voice trailed as he looked past her toward their car, towards the shadow walking towards them. "Marianne?" He stepped out of the porch in a trance-like state. "Marianne?" he whispered.

Astrid took advantage of this distraction to barrel through the door past George.

"Felton," said Marianne.

"It is you," said George. "It is you, isn't it?"

"We're here for the boy."

"My god-" he stammered. "I should have known you'd be behind this."

"—George." Regina's voice could be heard in the distance. "What's going on out there. What's all the noise?" She peered out the front door. "What is going on?" She squinted her eyes towards Marianne, then widened them immediately. "YOU!" Regina jabbed into George's back. "Get her out of here, George. Get her off my property! Get that *PUTA* out of my property!"

"Whoa! Glad to see you've found your Mexican roots girl. Relax, Gina," said Marianne tauntingly, "We're not here for you."

"What the hell are you even doing here," growled Regina. "Don't you dare let her in, George. What the hell is going on here! You need to get off my property!"

George remained motionless, his mouth dry and his eyes saucer-shaped in some unfathomable trance after seeing Marianne. He hadn't seen her in years. For a moment he couldn't tell if it was Marianne or her sister, Sarah, he was looking at. The similarity of their features was haunting.

Regina shoved her elbow into her husband's rib. "Get that trash right out of here. Get her out of here now! What are you waiting for?!"

Marianne stepped onto the front porch, her face a mask of anger. "Get a hold of yourself, Gina," she said, her voice low and menacing. "The only reason you landed my sister's sloppy seconds is because you found a witch dumb enough to help you. You think our family cursed your boy? My mother? She is the one who helped you when no one else would. You think we did this to your son? Cursed him with some unnatural love?" She leaned in closer to Regina, her voice rising. "We all know that you are no one to judge on matters of the heart. The heart wants what the heart wants," she said, her eyes blazing, "and even the strongest magic cannot deny its will. If love is a curse, then you're the most blessed woman in the world. You, Regina, are highly blessed."

Regina's mouth trembled as she clawed at her husband's frozen body. "Do something!" she spat.

George was about to speak up when Marianne said, "You don't deserve it, but we are here to save your son."

"Oh, you're not going to touch my son, you BITCH!" Regina was about to slap Marianne when they heard a loud gunshot discharge from the second floor of the Felton Rose.

They Look for Magic

ASTRID BOLTED UP THE stairs. She didn't even feel her feet when they pounded on the stairs leading up to Benny's room. She was terrified as thought after thought ricocheted in her mind. *THE BLOOD! It's in the blood!* There was nothing to be done. The last time she raced towards someone's room in the middle of the night, she found her mother sprawled on the floor of her bedroom, writhing, dying in agony. *It's in the blood!*

"Benny!" She hurled herself through the door with all her strength.

His back was turned to her. Even with all the commotion, he did not move a muscle. She nervously entered the room, looking towards the window and on the ground to make sure the Malinal snake was not around.

"Benny," her voice trembled. "Are you alright?"

Benny's hands were shaking, the gun quivering in his fingers. "I've never shot a gun before."

"Where is it? Where's the Malinal?"

Benny was unphased by the question and pointed to an area behind the curtains. There, curled in a tight ball, was the limp body of a blue rattlesnake.

"I saw it. Something told me to turn around," he said quietly. "Something was telling me to look at the window."

She held him. "I thought it was going to get you."

"I never open my windows," he said. "I don't know how it was even open."

She kicked the body and shut the window and locked it. Astrid reached for a dumbbell in the corner of the room and bashed the snake's head in. "Fucker," she hissed.

"How did you know it was here?" He asked, confused.

Astrid felt tears forming. "I have God's blood remember" she said. "I saw you. I saw that you needed me."

Benny smiled weakly. "I'm glad you did. I was going to do something I shouldn't have."

Astrid reached for his hands and squeezed them. "I know you were. I'm sorry about earlier. I shouldn't have been so mean to you. I don't know what came over me."

"I heard your voice," he explained. "That's what made me turn. That's what made me snap out of it."

"I was here," she affirmed. "I saw everything."

He nodded his head. "I know you were. I felt you. I couldn't see you. But I felt you."

She extended her arms and embraced him. "Let's take you home. You're not safe here."

He agreed, and the pair made their way down the stairs, where they saw Regina, George and Marianne arguing at the front door.

"Mom!" He called from the top of the stairs. "Enough!"

Everyone looked up the stairs.

"What was that sound!" demanded Regina.

"A gunshot," replied Benny in a matter-of-fact voice. "I killed a snake."

"A Malinal," said Astrid as they walked down the stairs.

Regina immediately turned away, her eyes shifting back and forth.

Marianne stepped inside the house. "Oh, Gina. Look at you, looking as guilty as sin." George backed away from Marianne. "Gina, Gina, Gina," she clicked her tongue. "What have you been up to?"

Regina backed away, hurling a chair in front of her. "Get out of this house," she screamed. "I didn't mean for this to happen. I didn't plan for any of this!"

"No one ever does." Marianne moved the sofa chairs with a flick of her finger.

"I swear! I just wanted to help my son!"

"Do you know what you've done?" Astrid and Benny stepped behind Marianne.

172

"I'm sorry!" Regina fell to the floor. "They told me to bring those goddamn snakes. That was part of the deal. They only agreed to take Benny if I agreed to it. I only did it because I thought that *she* had something to do with it. When I told them about Sarah, they said that I had to bring those snakes and leave them in a cemetery. They said they would cure Benny if I did it. They said they could fix him."

"I can't believe you actually thought my mom had something to do with Benny being gay? What is wrong with you?" screamed Astrid.

She looked away angrily. "I know she did! All of this... this... this magic. It turned him. It made him unnatural."

"Jesus, Gina," said Marianne, "I always knew you had a few loose screws, but goddamn, I didn't think you were bat shit crazy."

Regina raised her head in defiance. "It is not crazy to love one's child. You don't know anything about that since no one bothered to marry you."

"Well, you got me there. But it is crazy to think that magic can solve your problems." Marianne stepped closer. "You don't even know the shit-show you got into. What you got *us* into."

"What do you mean?"

"Those witches you went to see," stated Marianne. "You have no idea what they are capable of." Marianne lowered her sunglasses and pointed to her fake eye. "You don't play with those witches. The Witches of Cascabel will fuck you up."

"They said they would cure him."

"They killed my mother," screamed Astrid. "One of those snakes attacked her. That's what killed her."

"Your mother died of cancer," insisted Regina.

"You know that's not true, Regina. Deep down, you know you have something to do with her death. That's why you are having the novenarios here. That's why you paid for her funeral. You're about as transparent as a ghost. You brought the devil to this town."

Regina looked away without saying a word.

"How long have those snakes been here, Gina?"

Regina was shaking.

"How long have they been here," Marianne slapped her.

"I just dropped them off in the cemetery like they asked. It was a few days ago." Regina shook her head.

"How many snakes were there?"

"I don't know. They were in a suitcase. I left it in the cemetery like the man told me to."

"There's one upstairs right now. Do you know what those snakes hunt?"

"Hunt?"

"Yes, Regina. Hunt. They crawl on the ground, they smell, they search. They look for magic and then they bite."

"Why are they here? There's no magic in this house."

"You sure about that, Gina?" She turned to Benny.

After a brief moment of silence, Regina spoke. "What are you going to do to me?" she asked softly.

"Something was taken from us. We will take something from you."

"Take it. I have money. Take it."

"I'm taking Benny," said Marianne. "You don't love him either way."

"Of course I do!" she snapped.

"You don't," she said. "You love the idea of him. Those are two very different things."

"He's my baby," she pleaded.

"You should be ashamed of yourself, Regina," said Astrid.

Regina's mouth dropped. She pressed a hand against her chest. For the first time in a long while, Regina Felton was unable to speak. Her mouth fumbled and her lips writhed, but no words were able to form.

"And Sarah was my sister," she reached for Regina, her right hand wrapped around her thin neck. She pushed her against the wall and lifted her body easily. Regina's feet dangled inches above the ground and the room was quickly filled with the sound of sizzling flesh and the smell of sulfur. Marianne released her and her body landed with a thud.

"Sorry I couldn't be the son you wanted," Benny said. "But I'm still a good person. You can try to change me all you want, but the deepest part of me will always be good. Maybe that's the thing you hate the most. I'm not the

THEY LOOK FOR MAGIC

stain you think I am. Sorry, Regina, but to thine own self be true."

"Benny, don't go with those people." Regina looked up from the ground, her eyes wet with grief.

"I'm sorry, mom."

Marianne stared at the red palm print she had branded on Regina's neck. "Bless your heart," she winked as she walked out the door.

It broke Benny's heart to hear his mother's cry, but he also made his way through the doors of the Felton Rose one last time. He knew he could never return to such a grave house.

Being Brave

LAUREL HIGH SCHOOL was alive. It had been over two weeks since Astrid had been to school. The truth was that Astrid had no idea whether anyone was aware of her mother's death. The cut was still so fresh that she did not know how to handle being asked about it.

The yearbook teacher, Ms. Bunny, was standing by her door, talking with a student when she turned to Astrid and gave her the biggest hug ever. "I'm so sorry," she said before letting go. She rubbed the sides of her arm firmly. "I know. I know."

Astrid felt a lump in her throat but mustered a "thank you" before entering the room. She was about to start writing the daily journal down when she felt a pencil tap the side of her shoulder.

"Welcome back," said Dylan Arias as he pulled out a chair and sat next to her.

Astrid's heart fluttered. "Thanks."

"I heard about your mom," he said, "Sorry for your loss."

Astrid felt the lump in her throat again, and she felt her face turn red. All she could do was nod and fight back the tears.

"I don't know what I'd do if that happened to me. You're super strong."

"It's all I can be," she shrugged.

"You're like some sort of Superman. Well, Supergirl, I guess. You can survive it all."

"Everyone has their kryptonite," she said.

Dylan's eyes widened. "Damn. You know about Superman?"

"Who doesn't?"

"Cool. I like Superman, too. He's my favorite superhero."

"I didn't know that," she lied. "But I prefer Marvel superheroes more."

"Oh," he looked disappointed. "Well, everyone's got their fandom."

Ms. Bunny Broke their conversation abruptly.

"Alright, class, let's partner up for today's assignment. Astrid, why don't you stay with Mr. Arias? Go ahead and stay where you are," she nodded at Astrid. "Let's have one person, ONE person grab an SLR Camera and practice taking shots using the Rule of Thirds. Remember y'all, to put your subject into one of the intersections on the horizontal and vertical lines on your viewfinder. A lot of you all are STILL just putting your subject in the center. We want to add depth to our photos even if we are just practicing."

"Can we use our phones," asked Dylan. "I got a new phone, and I want to try it out."

"That's fine," said Bunny, "Astrid, your team can use your phones since I think we have a few cameras that weren't charged even though I constantly remind you all to charge them up."

"Stand up," said Dylan. "Let me take a picture of you by the window. It's good lighting."

"OK," Astrid reluctantly agreed and stood by one of the several windows lining the north side of the classroom.

"Smile," he raised his phone.

She did as instructed, fidgeting a bit with her hair and shifting her balance as he pointed his phone at her. Dylan snapped the photo then quickly inspected it. "Another one," he said.

"What's wrong with it?" Flashy. *He likes flashy—Not simple.* Astrid may be able to ride the wind, but in the real world, she was just basic.

"Uh, nothing," he flashed his pearly whites. "It's just that it's centered. I need a Rule of Thirds."

"Oh," she said. "Move the camera a bit. Remember, it's like a tic tac toe, and I need to be in one of the intersections."

"I know, I know. Just smile. I like your smile."

Astrid obliged, hoping the redness she felt on her face would not come out on camera.

"Wow. You look really pretty here."

Astrid felt her face flush. "It's just the lighting."

"No," he said as he got closer. "You do. It's not just the light," Dylan smiled and leaned in so only she could hear. "I've always thought you were pretty. No. Beautiful." He was quiet for a moment and eventually said, "I've always liked you." He cracked a smile and blushed. "Wow," he brushed his hair back and quickly turned away when their eyes met. "I can't believe I just said that."

Astrid didn't know what to say. What could she say? This information would have been useful BEFORE she walked into a burning sugar cane field. Before any of the crazy events of the past weeks had happened. She was left to ponder what might have been if she had never stepped foot in the Felton fields.

"You don't have to say anything," he shook his head playfully, then stuck out his lower lip. "Though, I wish I was brave like you," he said, continuing to look at the photos on his phone. His face suddenly turned white. "What the—" he said abruptly, bringing his phone closer. He zoomed in on a section of the photo he had just taken of Astrid. "What is that?" he said, his voice filled with confusion and curiosity.

"What is it? What's wrong?"

"By the window. Is that... Is that a snake?" He squinted his eyes as he handed back her phone.

Astrid's eyes widened when she saw the blue coiled snake resting on the window sill behind her in the photograph. It was staring right at her.

Dylan turned to the window. "I've never seen anything like that. It has a rattle at the end. Looks like a king snake, but with a rattler at the end."

The snake was still on the window sill, looking into the classroom. Suddenly Mrs. Bunny let out a hellish scream.

"S-snake!"

The whole class turned. Astrid stepped forward, and the snake perked its head.

"Astrid. What are you doing?" asked Dylan.

"Being brave," she said.

She stepped in front of it. The snake lifted its head until it was at her eye

178

level.

"Astrid! Get away from the window."

Astrid felt her heart pounding. "I'm not afraid of you," she whispered.

The animal attacked the window with five forceful strikes before it suddenly collapsed. A stream of blood ran down the glass. Astrid heard a crashing sound from behind her.

"Bruh," someone screamed. "Bunny fainted!"

The Croaking Raven

"DUDE!" BENNY WAVED his hands frantically as Astrid walked towards him. He had never been so glad to see his friend. It had been an adventurous day for him, and he was just waiting to see her come out of the main building to tell her all about it. "Tell me you've seen the yearbook teacher's fat ass thrown on the floor. Tell me you have! I've been making memes about it all day."

"That's not funny, Benny," Astrid smacked his shoulder. "She fainted, dumbass. She could have had a heart attack or something."

Benny cackled. "That's hilarious. It serves her right for being so damned *delicada*. Prissy old bag just face planted. God!" he roared. "I wish I could have seen it all. I would have live-streamed the hell out of it!"

"You didn't see the whole thing? It happened during my class period. It freaked everyone out. You didn't hear everyone screaming. I bet your ass would have been thrown on the floor, too."

"Damn. Well, what happened exactly. I only saw a video of Bunny on the floor."

"Dude! It was one of those Malinal snakes again! The one you shot in your room. They're everywhere!"

"Global warming, man."

Astrid scoffed. "It's not global warming, dummy. They're sending more. Don't you see that? And then when I got closer to one, it kind of stood up—"

"Snakes don't have legs, dummy."

"No, fool. The head. It raised itself. That's what I meant, and it looked right at me. Straight at me! Benny, it was so ugly! Then it began attacking

180

the window, just ramming and bashing its body against the glass. It wouldn't stop. It just kept hitting and hitting and hitting the glass until it cracked some of it. Its face was all smashed and bloody. It was horrible."

"Maybe it has some sort of disease. Like a zombie disease. Maybe it was trying to kill itself or something."

"No, Benny," snapped Astrid. "It wasn't trying to kill itself. It was trying to get inside. It was trying to get to me."

Marianne's car pulled up.

"We saw another one of those snakes," said Astrid before she closed the door.

Marianne shook her head. "Another one?"

"Yes!"

"I've only seen the one I shot."

"What was it doing?" Asked Marianne

"It looked like it was... spying."

"Spying?" said Benny. "How the hell can a snake be spying? Especially a blue one. One that stands out. Spies hide. Spies stay out of sight. That one smashed its head against the window."

Astrid nodded. "It's true. When I got close to the window, it attacked."

"Attacked."

Astrid nodded. "Yes! The janitor was saying he had never seen anything like it before. Like ever! Dylan said it looked like a combination between an indigo snake and a rattlesnake. It was a long one, too. Longer than the ones from before."

Marianne was quiet, but she tightened her grip on the steering wheel as they drove from Norton City towards Diller.

"It was just a snake, dude. You're reading too much into it. Marianne," said Benny. "Have you heard anything from my mom? She's not answering my texts. I want to let her know I'm OK, but I don't get a reply."

"No. I saw her pull up to the house earlier today. But she never got off. I don't know what she's up to."

"My dad went by the counselor's office today. They called me into their office, but once I saw he was there, I walked out."

"You need to talk to your parents, Benny. I don't mind you staying with us, but I don't want to be accused of kidnapping either."

"I'm not kidnapped. I am there of my own volition."

"Using AP words isn't going to cut it, Benny. I know you're mom's not right, but we can't risk Marianne getting into trouble. I just think that she needed time to cool off—"

Marianne suddenly hit the breaks.

She saw two Malinal snakes on the road leading to their house.

"Oh crap," said Benny. "There's more of them! What the hell is going on?"

Astrid turned to Marianne. "They're not going to stop, are they?"

The snakes slithered towards the car. They raised their heads as if scanning the perimeter.

"They are looking for us," said Astrid.

"They're looking for you," said Marianne.

"Me?"

She lowered her head and shook it. "They're just going to keep coming back."

"We need to stop them. I'm not going to live in fear." Astrid flared her nose. "Screw those snakes," she said to the two snakes as they slithered closer to the car. She turned to Marianne. "And screw those witches, too."

Marianne fixed her sunglasses.

"Screw those witches," she smiled.

Benny leaned in from the back of the car, "*The croaking raven doth bellow for revenge.*"

Marianne's face suddenly twisted. "Astrid, what the hell is this kid talking about?"

Astrid laughed and nodded her head intensely. "He means we're going to find those Witches of Cascabel."

Benny smacked the back of the seat. "Floor it, Girl," he roared.

Marianne grinned, tightening her grip on the steering wheel. She revved the engine and sped towards the two snakes and cackled when she heard their bodies thump below.

Epilogue

GEORGE FELTON'S TALL silhouette framed the doorway of the Cortez house.

"Never thought I'd see this again," said Marianne, walking to the door. "Little George Felton all grown up and back here looking for a Cortez girl."

"I'm not here for a girl. I'm here for my son."

"Same thing," she mocked.

George clenched his jaws. "Bring him out. I'm taking him home. I need to make sure he's OK. I have CPS on speed dial and I will press charges against you if you don't comply. He's a minor. You can't keep him here."

"He is free to go whenever he wants. But why would he go with you? Why would he ever go back to you? You lost him, Georgie. You and that bitch, Regina. You lost."

George lowered his head. "You people have been on the defensive your whole life. That's why it never worked out with Sarah. Everything gets scrutinized. Everything gets torn apart and picked at—everything we say offends you. Everything we say is an insult. Can't you just be civil? The world isn't out to get you. I'm not the bad one here, Marianne. I've always been on your side. You're the one that can't play by the rules."

"I'm not playing your game anymore, Felton. Get out of my house or I'll do something you won't like."

"What. You're going to set my house on fire. You're going to turn me into a toad. Kill me?"

"No. But I'll make you wish you were dead. I think it's ironic actually."

"What is?"

"A day before Sarah died, she told me that she went to visit our grandmother's old house. The one by the river, the one on Talavera Road. She said they were going to tear it down any time now to build a wall. She told me that she never realized how much she was going to miss that little old house. It wasn't much to look at but it was part of her. Her heritage. It's funny how we only start to appreciate things until we see them slipping away."

"What's your point?"

"That's kind of how you must feel. With Benny."

"He's not slipping away."

Marianne chuckled. "Baby, he's been bulldozing away from you and Regina for quite some time. And that wall, it's at least twelve feet tall by now. With barbed wires and all."

"Look, you can't make me feel any worse than I already do. Just get Benny for me."

"Oh, I think I can." She took a step forward. "I think I know just how to take my knife, press it firmly against your chest, and wiggle my way until I find a heart."

"You can't hurt me."

A wide grin formed across her face as she ran her fingers over his chest, "I know your secret. I may not be psychic but I know what you did."

His eyes widened. "Sarah wouldn't have."

"She didn't have to..."

He lowered his eyes.

She stepped back. "Leave the boy with me or I'll do what I have to. Let's call this payment for what Regina did. She took something from me. I'll take something from her."

"What am I supposed to tell her?" he extended his hands pleadingly. "Help me, Marianne. She feels terrible about this."

Marianne opened the screen door and set her foot inside the home. "Tell her the truth."

"I can't do that. You know I can't," he said.

"Then lie to her, Georgie. What's one more lie? After all, what's a Felton without his lies?"

His eyes became wet. "Don't hurt him. Please don't do him wrong."

"Baby, if your crazy wife didn't break him, nothing will."

"She's not a monster. She's just—"

"—Yes, she is. I don't judge you for loving a monster. Everyone has their flaws. I judge your weakness. It's done irrevocable damage."

"Tell him I love him."

"I'm not a messenger," she said, now speaking to him through the other side of the screen.

"Then let him see me if he wants. Do that for me at least."

"I will do what is best for his sake. Not yours."

"I do love him," said George. "I tried. I, I do."

"Then let him go."

"Tell Astrid," he put his hands on the screen door. "Tell her that we love her, too. She won't believe it, but tell her. We've got no ill will towards her. Tell her anyway."

Before she shut the door, Marianne smiled and said, "Of course you do. What father wouldn't love his daughter?"

The Story Continues

ASTRID CORTEZ AND THE WITCHES OF CASCABEL

Made in United States
Orlando, FL
02 November 2023

38514865R00107